MARY HORROR

By

Nick Kisella

Based on the screenplay by

Ryan Scott Weber

First printing

A Weber Pictures Novel

Cover Art By Chris Waters
Nick Kisella's photo by Stan Stronski
Ryan Scott Weber's photo by Michael Enoches

Dedications

Nick Kisella:

Kim, always my heart and best friend.
Nicholas Richard and Kimberly Gayle; you both make me
smile-
even when I don't want to.
Here's another one Rich-

Ryan Scott Weber:

To my best friend, JC. You are missed every day.

Mom, Dad, Travis, Kristen and Tom,

for supporting me and all my crazy ideas.

PRELUDE

My life was once peaceful and innocent,
just like everyone expects life to be.
But now, I'm different...

The yellow house stood out like a beacon in the night. To Mary Horowitz, the pale yellow two-story Victorian was salvation from the overwhelming pain and deep sense of betrayal that she felt in her heart. It was a warm comforting escape from the tears that stung her eyes on that cold dark fall night. She flung the mess of her long dark hair back out of her face, pulled her jacket closed and jumped out of her car. She slammed the car door shut much harder than she'd intended without even realizing it, her eyes focused on her home.

Mary tried to suppress a sob when she realized how clear the night was, which she noticed because the stars cast shadows that shouldn't have been there. The lights outside the house would have made sure of that, as they always had; but oddly, they weren't on. The thought crossed her mind for a second, but then the utter sadness she felt took hold again and she abandoned the thought of starlight and shadows, thinking only of how her world had been utterly shattered.

Her heart was racing as she trudged up the cobbled driveway, and even though she started running after a couple of strides, it felt like forever before she reached the steps leading to the front door. All she could think of was how she needed the door to be open, so she wouldn't have to struggle through her pocket for a key, and just get inside where she could collapse. So she could get inside and fall into a heap that her Mom's arms could wrap around and comfort somehow. Her Mom was always able to take her pain away, but Mary was afraid. She was afraid that this time, her pain was something only she could deal with, and that thought of being alone with it made her even more upset and she flung herself through the door, her body pressed firmly against it as it shut.

"Mom?" She said with a sob. She looked around quickly, and saw that there were no lights on. "Mom, are you home?"

She needed her to be home. She needed to not be alone.

"Mom, I need to talk to you!" Mary pleaded to the silence.

She stepped away from the door and let her eyes adjust to the dim light cast through the windows. There was a soft droning sound, as if the television was on, so she looked over her left shoulder, toward the living room. The television screen was snowy, as if the cable box had been shut off, but there, in the murky light, she saw him.

She saw a man, dressed in black from head to toe, wearing a ski mask. Her heart pounded even harder in her chest when she realized he was standing over her mother, who was lying on the floor. Her throat had been slit and dark red blood still throbbed out of the wound, covering her chest.

Mary gagged, and tried to scream, but all she could get out was a muffled cry as she looked around the room in a panic. Across the room she saw her brother sitting on the couch, covered in his own blood from a wound similar to her Mom's. Mary's eyes went wide and her lips trembled when she saw her father lying just a few feet to her left. She took a step back and nearly tripped on her own feet.

He was still alive, but bleeding.

"Mary!" His voice was a low rasping sound, and he tried to raise his arm, but collapsed from the effort.

The sound of her father's voice snapped her out of the terror that had seized control and she screamed. She screamed more loudly than she ever had before in her life.

The man in black, holding a cleaver covered in blood, lunged toward her, but he was too late. Mary twisted around and ran. She shoved through the front door and leaped the steps, screaming and running into the woods that surrounded the house.

She could hear the man following her. He was close, his steps loud and pounding in her ears, drowning out the sound of her own sobs. She ran as fast as she could, recklessly weaving between trees as he chased her into the darkness of the woods.

"Shit, shit, shit!" Mary shouted, barely skirting around a thick oak tree. "Help! Somebody help!" She screamed, fearing that the woods would stifle the sound.

Mary's lungs burned, but she forced herself to speed up in spite of the pain she felt with every gasp. When she was certain that she'd lost her pursuer, she ducked down behind a thick tree. Clinging to the shadows, she began to breathe solely through her nose, trying to be as quiet and still as possible.

Her mind had a second to wander, and tears began to fill her eyes, but her thoughts were abruptly cut off with the echo of movement nearby.

The footsteps she heard were sudden, and closer than she wanted them to be. Mary held her breath and waited for them to pass with each heartbeat feeling like forever. After a minute or so more, she quietly pushed herself to her feet and peered around the tree.

There was no one in sight.

Mary turned and bolted, heading back toward her house, hoping to reach her car or at least the cell phone she'd carelessly left inside her purse on the passenger seat.

The leaves crackled overly loud in her head, sounding like thunder, and the exposed tree-root in her path was completely covered in them when she tripped up on it. It happened so fast that

Mary didn't even have a chance to cry out as her face slammed into the ground.

"Damn it!" Mary whispered harshly and punched the ground.

She fumbled for a second, and tried to get to her feet.

The footsteps came out of nowhere, and suddenly the man in black, the walking shadow, stood directly in front of her. She could see the starlight reflect off his shiny black shoes and when she looked up, the blade of the cleaver seemed to glow as the man raised it high in the air.

A second later she saw it coming down at her.

Mary felt sudden agony explode in her belly as the breath rushed out of her lungs and the wet sound of a watermelon being smashed echoed through the trees.

Darkness claimed her.

ONE

I may appear to look the same, but I feel,
I feel different.
The pain almost feels good.
It's better than anything I've ever felt before.

It was close to midnight at Morristown Memorial Hospital, and though the night had been quiet, it was still early. Doug Rowlans was a middle-aged security guard. About to begin his shift, he paced just outside the doors to the emergency room puffing on a thick cigar, admiring the clear night before he started work.

"The crazy shit doesn't start up until way after midnight," he mumbled, exhaling a thick cloud of rich smelling smoke, "when the bars close up."

Suddenly the screaming siren of an ambulance pierced the serenity of the night.

"Damn!" Rowlans said, taking one last deep puff. He tossed away his cigar as soon as he saw the pulsing lights of the vehicle as it sped into the lot. The brakes to the ambulance squealed and it swerved to a halt. Doug rushed over and flung open the back doors to help the EMTs.

In seconds the doors to the emergency room split open with a pneumatic hiss and Doug was there with three EMTs carrying in a stretcher. The three of them carefully lowered it onto a gurney and quickly wheeled it into the emergency room.

Mary, curled into a fetal position, clutched at a thick pad of gauze that covered a growing deep red blot in the center of her lower abdomen. Her face was stained with blood and tears and she shuddered with pain. She tried to lie back, and with a shriek of agony, succeeded, suddenly dizzy from the exertion.

"Oh my god, it hurts so much!" she cried, visibly trembling as she was pushed further into the hospital. Her thoughts flooded with the images of her family and how they had died so brutally. She couldn't get the sight of her mother's face, the bloody slash across her throat, out of her mind. Mary suddenly felt ice cold, and her body, all of her muscles clenched up involuntarily.

A doctor and a pair of nurses raced toward the gurney.

"Talk to me Bobby!" The doctor said, nodding to the nearest EMT as he and the nurses took control of the gurney and began to examine Mary.

"Dr Hess, we have a female in her late teens, possibly early twenties." Bobby said, out of breath.

"She's got a gash, roughly five to seven inches across her lower abdomen." Billy, the EMT at the far end of the gurney said.

"Was she attacked or something?" Hess asked.

Billy shrugged; an uncertain look on his face and a fine coat of sweat beading up on his forehead as he struggled to keep up.

"We're not sure what happened." Bobby said. "We got the call anonymously and found her in the woods by her house."

"The Sheriff was on his way there to check on things when we picked her up." Billy chimed in.

"Well, I hope they catch whoever did this." Hess replied, nodding toward the wound.

*****

Sheriff Tom Walker, 'Sheriff Tom' to his friends, passed the ambulance with Mary in it while on his way to the Horowitz house near the center of Bernardsville. As he pulled into the driveway he saw that the house was dark. He snatched up a flashlight from the glove compartment of the patrol car and got out to check the house for anything unusual.

The front door was wide open, so Sheriff Tom shined the light right inside. There were a few drops of blood on the floor, and they looked fresh. He walked further in and saw more blood leading into the living room. When he shined the light across the room and saw the bodies strewn about, his eyes widened; three people, bloodied and dead.

"Holy fucking shit!" The Sheriff stammered, walking back outside to the porch. He pulled out his hand-held radio, took a deep breath and tried to think of what he would tell dispatch. For a second he was totally at a loss, and took a deep breath. He lifted off his hat, rubbed his smooth scalp, and just started talking. "I'm at the Horowitz place. You'd better send all the boys down here for this one," he said, after getting through to his deputy. "There's blood and bodies everywhere, almost the entire family, dead. We're gonna need forensics here tonight too, while everything is still fresh."

Sheriff Tom saw Mary's car parked in the driveway close to the house. He walked over to it and decided to check it out. There wasn't much inside, though for some reason her purse was there. Her keys were even still in the ignition. The Sheriff took them out, tossed them in the purse and then noticed an old looking book lying on the passenger seat. He lifted it up, feeling the rough binding and cover, as if it were made of some type of animal skin. There was an odd symbol on the front cover. It was drawn in red, blood-red. A flyer for the missing girl, Kelly Slater, was lying under it.

"What the hell?" He said, skimming through some of the books pages. "This looks like some sort of witchcraft."

*****

Dr. Hess slid a pair of scissors out of the top pocket of his lab coat and began cutting away at the lower part of Mary's shirt. He tried to pull away the gauze to expose the wound but Mary, weak and delirious, fought against his probing hands.

"She's lost a lot of blood." Jimmy, the third EMT said. "I don't know how she's still conscious."

"Please!" Hess said sternly, holding onto Mary's struggling hands. "I need to look at the wound."

"Stop it!" Mary shouted, wild-eyed. "Please just leave me alone!"

Hess grasped her chin and gently turned her face toward him so he could look directly into her eyes.

"You're safe! Calm down! I want to help you, but I can't if you won't let me!" The doctor said firmly but quietly.

Mary continued to struggle but eventually gave in when weakness overcame her.

"What's your name?" Dr. Hess asked, finally able to pull the blood soaked gauze away from her clutching hands.

Mary didn't respond, but Billy, still standing next to Hess, pulled out the call sheet. He squinted to read the tiny lettering. "Her name is Mary Horowitz."

Abruptly, Mary screamed at the sound of her own name. Dr. Hess pulled back his hands, wide-eyed. He looked at the nurses that were following closely.

"Sedate her immediately and prep her for surgery." He said, standing still as Mary was wheeled away. "I'll be in there with her as soon as I scrub."

Mary screamed again as she was wheeled further down the hall. Dr. Hess sees her raise a bloody hand, clutching at the air, as if she were trying to grab something. Confused, he shakes his head and leaves to scrub for what he guesses will be a long arduous surgery.

*****

Outside the hospital, the press had already begun to gather, attempting to get any information possible regarding the murders.

"Good evening ladies and gentlemen, we're here live outside Morristown Memorial Hospital in Bernardsville, I'm Chuck Marble. As you may know, something happened here in town last night that has never happened before in the history of Bernardsville. A family brutally murdered in their own home. There is one known survivor, the daughter, Mary Horowitz who is in the hospital here tonight. We are joined now by two EMTs who attended to Mary tonight as she was brought in." He turns toward the EMTs, who are both smiling.

"She's dead." Jimmy said, totally serious.

"She is dead." Marble repeated.

Billy, who was smiling next to him quickly rolled his eyes and sighed, annoyed.

"She's not dead," He said to the reporter, frustrated. He turns to Jimmy, shaking his head at him. "Why do you always say everybody's dead," he pushed Jimmy, "what's wrong with you?" Billy knocked Jimmy down and started cursing at him. The curses were of course bleeped out by the news channel as the pair started throwing punches at each other. The scene rapidly became a battle one might see in a rerun of the 'Three Stooges', less one Stooge.

"You say my mom's dead, you say my dad's dead, my grandma's dead." Billy goes on, punching Jimmy while holding him on the ground. "No one's dead, man, no one!" He punches him one more time, "You're fucking dead!" which was the only curse the network missed, and would eventually be fined for.

"Okay," Marble said, watching the two get up off the ground, out of breath. "Well obviously some misinformed EMTs there." Suddenly Marble sidesteps to avoid Billy, who was jumped by Jimmy, and the two begin to scuffle again.

"*Our sources on the inside say that Mary is here in the hospital and that she's in stable condition. Doctors are attending to her. As far as the investigation is concerned, efforts are ongoing to find the suspect. There have not been any suspects named at this time.*"

Billy and Jimmy both stop fighting and get to their feet.

"*I'm sorry buddy,*" *Billy said, putting his arm around Jimmy's shoulders.* "*Let's go to JC's Pub and have a drink.*"

Chuck Marble can only roll his eyes and continue his broadcast as the pair stroll away.

"*The police are chasing down all leads. We're live in Bernardsville, I'm Chuck Marble. We'll see you again at eleven.*"

TWO

Mary was jarred awake by pain. Her head hurt, throbbed with every beat of her heart, and her stomach was sore in a weird way. She felt her forehead and found that there was a bandage there.

"Huh?" She mumbled, not remembering where she was or how she got there. When she sat up, the stabbing pain in her lower abdomen brought the memories, the harsh reality of her current situation, slamming into her like a freight train.

She was lying in a hospital bed, a tube painfully taped to her arm, wires stuck to her chest to keep the heart monitor next to her bed beeping. The blinds that covered the sole window in the room were partially open, exposing the first light of dawn.

"Oh my god!" She cried, squeezing her eyes tightly shut against the tears that threatened to fall. "They're all dead!" Mary gripped her forehead with her hands, ignoring the ache it caused to the wound there.

Unable to deal with it, she forced herself to think of something else, anything, just to get her mind away from the pain of seeing her family murdered, and watching her own gut get ripped open by a cleaver. She couldn't cope with any of it now, and needed an escape more than anything else in the world.

It was Atlantic City that came to her mind first. The boardwalk with the scent of the ocean on the breeze, and the way the wind tossed her hair even on a cloudy day. She always loved it there.

Her thoughts drifted back a short time, and she remembered the day she met Madam Ruth. It was chilly that afternoon, but beautiful as always. Mary was sitting on a bench on the boardwalk reading through the book of spells she had recently received as a gift from her grandmother. She wasn't well versed in witchcraft, nor was she accustomed to reading things written in Old English, so each page was a frustrating learning experience in itself. The knowledge that her grandmother was into witchcraft was also a jarring thought. She would never have expected such a thing.

It was there, pondering it all, with what felt like an immense weight on her shoulders, that she met the old woman. She felt an odd chill run up her spine, looked up from her book and suddenly Madam Ruth was there, standing right in front of her, smiling like the cat that got the canary.

"You look upset, confused my dear," Madam Ruth said, the hint of a European accent in her voice. She sat down on the bench beside her. Mary saw that though her face was wrinkled with age her eyes were lively and bright.

"I suppose I've got a lot on my mind." She replied with an uneasy grin.

"Would you like me to read your fortune?" Madam Ruth asked, her eyes brightening even more, as if she were thrilled by her own words.

"How much does it cost?" Mary smiled eagerly, a tinge of excitement curling her lips into a smile.

"Well usually twenty dollars. Would you like to know your destiny?" Madam Ruth asked with a crooked smile.

"Sure." Mary replied. She pulled the cash out of her back pocket and slipped it into Madam Ruth's hands.

"Okay, so let me read you." She grinned and accepted the money, stuffing it into the pocket of her thick coat.

Madam Ruth took Mary's left hand and held it palm up between both of her own. She closed her eyes and grinned. "There's a change coming soon, a crossroads." She paused, tilting her head sideways, as if searching for the right words, then her expression straightened. "There might be danger ahead. Choose wisely." Her words were suddenly louder, stern with caution.

Madam Ruth released Mary's hand and opened her eyes in stunned alarm. Taking a deep breath, she looked down at Mary's other hand and saw the spell book. She looked at Mary curiously, but with concern.

"Where did you get that?" She said, gesturing to the book.

"It's a spell book." Uncomfortable with the way Madam Ruth is looking at the book, she tries to cover it up. "It was my grandmother's. Every since my best friend-"

"Your best friend," Madam Ruth said, cutting her off abruptly, "Something has happened to her hasn't it?"

"How did you know?" She said, dumbfounded. "Yeah, I was hoping the reading would help and maybe it could tell me where she is. I haven't been the same since she's been gone. No one knows where she is or what happened to her. What else can you tell me?" Mary leaned forward in anticipation.

Madam Ruth leaned back, her eyes narrowing on the cover of Mary's book.

"You must get out of this place!" Madam Ruth demanded suddenly angry, dashing Mary's hopes away. "I cannot have that book or that symbol within my sight. If you don't get rid of that book," she angrily shook her thin frail index finger in Mary's face, "bad things are going to happen!"

"What about my friend?" Mary asked, panicked. She stared at the book fearfully. "I can't get rid of this, it's my grandmother's. It means a lot to me."

Eyes wide and clearly distressed by what the woman had said, Mary stood from the bench. She held the book tightly against her chest, as if it was something that needed protection. "Okay, I'll go." Her words were barely above a whisper. She turned and ran away from the old woman, confused. She didn't know what to believe and it scared her.

Madam Ruth remained seated at the bench, a nervous expression on her face while she followed Mary with her eyes. She stood up suddenly, just as Mary turned to look back at her in the distance.

"I haven't seen that evil symbol in years!" The old woman said, shaking a clenched fist at Mary. "You be careful girl! Be very careful!" She shouted, pointing at her in forewarning.

Mary's thoughts returned to the present, the vivid image of Madam Ruth and her stern warning still in the back of her mind. She suddenly found herself afraid that the book had somehow caused all of the tragedy she and her family had experienced during the course of the last day.

"I might be responsible for everything just because I kept the book. But, how can that be?" She thought back to earlier in the day, after school, when she briefly met with her boyfriend.

Her 'boyfriend'; how she dreaded that word and the face behind it. Mark Silva, he was a jock in every sense of the word and he was her first real love. A mixture of fury and sadness filled her, but she thrust the feelings aside in an attempt to preserve her memory of the good times. The last time she had seen him, it was all still so fresh in her head.

The school day had just ended. She was sitting outside the gym, near the student parking lot, totally focused on her grandmother's book when he snuck up behind her.

"Boo!" He shouted, laughing as Mary jumped and shrieked.

"Don't do that!" She yelled, playfully slapping him.

"Hey, it was worth it to see you jump." Mark laughed.

"Walk me to my car?" She asked. "I have to be home early, I have this psychiatry appointment that I have to go to."

"Oh, that's exciting." Mark said with a chuckle. He hung his arm around Mary's shoulders and the pair walked to the parking lot.

"I'm really not looking forward to it." Mary said.

"Well, you shouldn't be. I don't like the idea of anyone getting in a person's head." Mark stared directly into her eyes. "Is it worth it? Is it helping you?"

"I don't know," she replied, shaking her head. "I don't want to talk about it. What are you going to be doing?"

"Um, I've got to run inside, talk to the coach before the game, so we can get our shit together." He said with a smile.

"Okay, well, I love you," she pulled him close when they reached her car and kissed him, "See you later."

She could still remember the scent of his aftershave.

"I love you too." Mark said, walking away after kissing her.

They said their goodbyes. Mary remembered it well. She also remembered seeing Sheriff Tom, in his crisp uniform as usual, posting 'Missing' signs for her best friend Kelly Slater all around the school that day.

THREE

All it took was the disappearance of my best friend Kelly.
That's what led me to see Dr. Connie Baxter.
My mother came along out of a sense of parental neglect.
It only took a few minutes for me to realize
That she needed someone to bitch to
As much as I needed a shoulder to cry on.

Dr. Connie Baxter, a middle aged psychiatrist, had lost the thrill regarding her profession years ago. It wasn't that she felt bored; she just really didn't care anymore. After so many years, and so many hurt people coming to see her, she realized that most of them would never get any better. She realized that most of them just came to see her to bitch and complain about life. They never really did anything to actually change things other than try to con her into prescribing medication for them.

When Mary and her mother had arrived on time for their appointment, she casually took some notes to begin with, just general information, then sat silently, drumming her fingers on the armrest of her chair, deciding on how to begin the session.

"So Mary, you seem to be fine from a psychological standpoint." Dr. Baxter said, leaning back into her chair to straighten her glasses. "But you haven't really told me anything about the night terrors your mother mentioned when she made the appointment. These have been happening since your friend has gone missing?"

"Yeah." Mary said dismissively. "I'm still having them, but I don't know what I'm supposed to tell you other than it's the same dream every night." Mary sat up in her chair nervously. "I'm with Kelly, she's my best friend. We're in the woods walking, talking about a book I got from my grandmother. Everything is fine, and then all of a sudden out of nowhere, she's abducted by a-" Mary couldn't think of how to describe what she saw in her dream. She shut her eyes and shook her head.

"What is she abducted by?" Dr. Baxter asked, suddenly knowing that Mary wasn't her typical patient. She wanted to smile because she finally felt she might be able to do some real good for a person.

"I can't explain it." Mary said, sighing loudly. Her mother, a sad expression on her face, began to absently stroke her hair.

Dr. Baxter took off her glasses and leaned forward.

"Just give it a shot Mary. Tell me whatever you can." She was happily feeling genuine concern and went with it. "The more you give me the more chance I have of being able to help you."

"Well, it's like I said, difficult to describe. It has no recognizable face or any sort of thing anyone can see. It's like the air just pulls her out of existence. One minute I'm with her and the next I can see her running, screaming as if she's being chased, and then she's gone. That's usually when I wake up screaming."

*****

Mark didn't feel the slightest bit guilty as he walked back into the school. He in fact, had a spring in his step and a smile on his face. He wasn't going to see the coach.

"Kimberly, here I come!" He mumbled with a wide grin. Mary was his neighbor and a nice girl. Sure, he liked spending time with her sometimes and enjoyed having sex with her on occasion, especially knowing he'd taken her virginity, but that was it. She lived close, so it was convenient. Mark wanted more, and being a star football player meant he could have it too. It didn't matter to him what Mary thought, because she was just Mary.

Mark headed to his locker, where Kim Fines, his blonde bombshell cheerleader was supposed to meet him before the game. His lower lip twitched with anticipation. As always, he couldn't wait to get his hands on her.

When he saw her his heart sped up just a little bit.

"Hey," He came up behind her and whispered in her ear.

Kim jumped at the surprise then laughed.

"You can't keep doing that," she said playfully making an angry face at him.

"So are you coming over before the game?" Mark asked.

"Hmm, I'm not sure," Kim replied.

Mark moved closer to her, his eyes locking onto hers.

"Please? Mary's not going to be around. She's going to a psychiatrist appointment with her mother."

"Maybe." Kim said with uncertainty.

"Come on!" Mark urged, covering her lips with a series of tiny kisses. Kim finally gave in and kissed Mark passionately.

A short distance down the hall, Fred Slater and George Grafton stand at their lockers, watching Mark and Kelly. Fred, a skinny geek to most, had an angry look on his face, while George look on in disbelief.

"He's cheating on Mary with that sparkle bitch! Mary, my sister's best friend! If Kelly wasn't still missing, if she were here-" Fred said furiously. "That fuckin' asshole!" He slammed his locker shut and turned to George.

"That is really fucked up." He agreed.

Fred stormed away angrily, leaving George standing there alone, still watching Mark and Kim.

*****

"I understand that living in the woods scares you now, especially with Kelly missing, but these dreams you have scare me." Arleen Horowitz, Mary's mother said, concerned. She looked at Dr. Baxter, and spoke directly to her. "My husband Jeff wanted a house in the country, the woods, because it was rustic and still close to town." Arleen turned toward her daughter. "It works out for all of us though. Your father gets his access to nature, I get the original wood flooring and molding of an old Victorian, and you," she rubbed Mary's shoulder and smiled, "well you get Mark." She looked at Dr. Baxter. "He's the boyfriend next door."

"Mary, a friend disappearing, especially in the manner that your friend Kelly has, would be difficult for anyone to deal with, no matter what age they are or where they live. Mom, you certainly seem attentive." Dr. Baxter said, nodding to Arleen, then turned to Mary. "How is Dad helping out?" She asked.

Mary thought back to what her father had said to her; how harshly he spoke to her, when he and her mother showed up at the high school unexpectedly after classes ended. It was a nightmare. She cringed inside when she thought of how he angrily complained to her about falling grades, never being home for dinner anymore, and how she had been spending way too much time with Mark. 'Like he has room to talk with as much time as he spends at home,' she thought with a tinge of bitterness.

"Dad's working on some big project with the Mayor and the Sheriff, so we really don't ever see him." Mary turned toward her mother, who was silent and looking down. "Well, we're supposed to rent a movie tonight and have a family night."

Dr. Baxter nodded. Still leaning forward, she noticed that Mary was holding something on her lap. 'The last thing I need is for Mary to be distracted by something she brought with her,' she thought to herself.

"Mary," she asked, sounding annoyed. "What are you holding?"

"You should show her, show her that book." Arleen said, catching Mary's eye.

"Ah, well," Mary pulled the book off of her lap and held it up. "As you know, I grew up in Salem, and before I moved to New Jersey my grandma asked to see me."

The last time she saw her grandma and spent time with her flashed through her mind before she could even begin to tell Dr. Baxter about the book. The memory played itself out in her mind as if she were living it again.

Mary was at her grandma's house. She remembered leaning on the counter in her kitchen while she was slicing up tomatoes for a salad they were going to share.

"Now Mary, here's how tomatoes should look after you cut them up," her grandma told her, "but don't cut your fingers."

"I know grandma." Mary laughed.

"I'm so afraid of what's going to happen when you move away." She put the knife she held down on the counter and looked at Mary. "You're going to be so far away."

"I don't want to move away either grandma, I don't have a choice though." Mary said. "It's Dad's idea."

"I do have a gift for you though." She turned away from Mary and walked to a narrow closet right by them.

"You do?" Mary said, surprised.

"It's right over here." She opened the closet and inside there was a wooden box. The lid of the box had an odd red symbol painted on it. The symbol looked like two letter M's crisscrossing each other. She flipped open the lid to the box and there was a purple cloth covering something. It was tied with a gold colored sash. "It's a family heirloom." She untied the sash and pulled an ancient looking book out of the purple cloth. The same symbol that was on the box was also on the cover of the book.

"Wow, that's amazing." Mary said, excited about the mysterious looking book.

"This has been in our family for many generations, and it's been passed on from one woman to the next." She held the book up then handed it to Mary. "It originally belonged to a distant relative of yours. Her name was Rebecca. She was persecuted during the Salem witch trials."

"Really?" Mary accepted the book from her grandma, thrilled, with eyes wide and even more curious than before.

"Yes. She was one of the witches they hanged."

"Oh my goodness," Mary said, sounding breathless. "That's terrible!"

"This book, according to my grandmother, was found in this box, in this house, fifty years after her death. It's a book of spells."

"Do they work?" Mary inquired, excited at the mere thought of learning how to cast spells that actually worked.

"They do, but you need to practice to get the results that you want." Her grandma said, hugging her. "I'm so sorry you're leaving."

Mary returned to the present and halfheartedly began telling Dr. Baxter about the book and her grandma.

"So my grandmother gave me this book," Mary said reluctantly. "And she said it was really special."

Dr. Baxter was staring at her intently, jotting down notes.

"I really loved her." Mary choked back a sob. "She died a few weeks ago. With the disappearance of Kelly, this book is really important. I guess you can say it's become sort of a security blanket."

"She's even doing a school project with it." Arleen said, sounding proud of her daughter and yet sad for all the loss she'd recently had to cope with.

"It's really good to have something to remember your grandmother by." Dr. Baxter said, reassuringly. Her watch caught her eye and she put her glasses back on to look at the time. "On that note, our time is about up for today. I will see you both again next week."

Arleen fumbled for her purse, trying to pull out her car keys while standing up. She felt tired, worn out emotionally from listening to Mary, and also drained from empathizing with her for the first time in months.

Mary walked to the door and waited for her mom.

"If you'll just speak with Janice at the front desk on your way out, she'll set you up with another appointment and also validate your parking for the month. That way you won't have to do it each time you're here." Dr. Baxter said, holding the door open for them. "Enjoy the movie tonight."

"I need to speak with you if you don't mind." Arleen said when she got to the door.

"I'm going to wait in the hall Mom," Mary said, rushing out and closing the door behind her.

"Mary, please let me know how that new prescription works out." Dr. Baxter said, quietly pushing the door shut.

"You seemed a slightly nervous today Arleen. Is everything really alright at home?" Dr. Baxter asked.

"Everything is fine." Arleen said. She pointed to the door and began to whisper. "I just didn't want to say anything while Mary was in here." Her expression became sad, and for a second she stared at the floor, nearly embarrassed to say what she was going to say. "I found something, in my husband's pocket."

"Don't be afraid to tell me," Dr. Baxter said reassuringly.

"Well, it wasn't Cinderella's glass slipper. It was panties. It was women's panties, and they're not mine." Arleen took a step back, clearly upset.

Dr. Baxter took her hand.

"Child psychology is my specialty. If you need someone for couples therapy I can recommend Dr. Howard."

"Sure, okay, I'll call you and maybe we can set something up for next week." She rushed her words, more nervous about what she'd said then she'd expected.

"My best advice for you is to not discuss this with Mary at all." Dr. Baxter said.

"Of course not. I would never bring her in the middle of this, especially with all she's going through herself." Arleen let herself out.

Mary stood there, right outside the door. She didn't say anything, but she'd heard everything her mother had said. She wanted to tell her that she was there for her, but decided against it. There was too much going on between everyone. She want to laugh out loud when she thought that maybe a 'family night' was really what they all needed. A good movie and some time to kick back and relax would do everyone some good.

The drive home was uneventful. Both women were tired, and neither of them wanted to talk anymore. When they got home, Mary's mother pulled her aside before they walked inside.

"You know, you have to be careful with that book Mary." She said sternly.

"I know. Grandma told me it was special." Mary replied, frustrated that her mother would even entertain the idea that she'd be careless with it.

"I'm talk more about the cash value than the content. You know, your grandmother was a good woman, and I loved her very much, but she wasn't 'all there', even in the best of times."

"Sure Mom." Mary shook her head and just walked in the house. She was angry with her mother for what she said, but she also felt bad for her for what she was going through. "So what were you talking to Dr. Baxter about anyway?" She turned to face her mother as she came inside behind her.

"None of your business." Her mother said, embarrassed. "Insurance stuff."

"Okay." She said in disbelief. She held up her grandmother's book. "I'm going to try to get through as much of this as I can, then I'm going to the game around seven."

"Honey, I know how much you've been looking forward to Homecoming. You've been looking forward to this for weeks, and I just want you to have a good time. So listen," she pulled a plastic bag out of her purse and dropped in onto the books Mary carried. There were two bottles of medication in the bag. "Here are your meds, bring them up to your bathroom so you remember to take them, and your dress for the dance tomorrow is already hanging on the back of the door."

"Thanks Mom, I'll let you know when I'm leaving." Mary smiled at her mother before walking up to her room. She knew her mother was right; she was really looking forward to Homecoming. She wanted everything to be perfect when she went to the dance with Mark.

A couple of hours later Mary was dressed and on her way out the door.

"Okay, bye Mom," She yelled, hopping down the stairs.

"Goodbye Mary, and remember to be on time for family night." She heard her mother reply. "And please be careful."

"I will Mom." Mary shook her head smiling as she made her way outside.

FOUR

Parking was close to impossible at the school. Homecoming was always crowded. Aside from the Thanksgiving game it was the biggest game of the season; practically the entire town attended.

Mary walked to the field as the sun was going down. The lights were already on so the area was very well lit and there were groups of students hanging around the field. She could see the cheerleaders practicing on the track. They were a highly competitive team and had already won several awards that year. The football players were warming up a short distance away from them. Mary spotted Mark, and they waved at each other.

She held back the excitement she felt and flipped open the spell book while continuing on to the bleachers. 'I guess I can probably get through a couple more pages before the game starts,' she thought to herself.

She spotted Fred and George handing out 'Missing' flyers for Fred's sister, her best friend. The sadness she suddenly felt was nearly overwhelming. Her friend was still missing and there weren't even any leads that she knew of. It scared her that a person she had been so close to, spent time with just about every day, had simply vanished as if she'd never existed.

"Hey Mary." Fred nodded as she approached them. "If you're looking for Mark, he's on the field already. The whole team just passed right by us."

"So, uh, how's the search going?" Mary said hesitantly. She always found herself tongue-tied around Fred, but could never figure out why. Ever since Kelly had been missing it had just gotten worse.

"The search is going great," George chimed in. "I just hope the Sheriff doesn't find her because then he's going to walk around thinking he's fuckin' Robocop, that small dick piece of shit cop."

"Why'd you have to mention the butterfly tattoo?" Mary said after reading over the flyer. She frowned. "Your parents are gonna flip!"

"Every little bit helps." Fred replied dryly. "There are bigger things to worry about. I'd rather have her home and in trouble for the ink than still missing."

"Yeah, bigger things to worry about," George smiled, "like hot chocolate. I'm outta here!"

Mary and Fred watched him walk away and then looked at each other. It was a very awkward silence between them.

"If you're looking for Mark, he's over there with all the other assholes." Fred broke the silence, reminding her with a quick gesture toward the field.

"Thanks, good luck." Mary grinned sadly and started to walk away. "See ya later."

Mary spotted the mayor leaning against a set of bleachers that hadn't been opened yet. He was staring at the cheerleaders as they practiced some of their newer moves.

Mayor Joe Grafton was short, a little past fifty, and always wore a cowboy hat. He acted like a maverick and thought of the town as his property. Sometimes he tended to make his own rules for handling things, economic or otherwise, even when the laws didn't allow it. No one ever questioned it because his best friend and right-hand man was Sheriff Tom.

Grafton saw Mary approaching and cursed to himself, not wanting to deal with her when there were so many cute skirts flying around in front of him. He knew all she wanted was information about her missing friend, and there was nothing he was willing to tell her about yet.

"Hi Mary," he smiled and pushed his hat up a little on his forehead. "What can I do for you?"

"Can you, do you have any information about Kelly's case?" Mary was nervous, her words a jumble in her throat. She wanted to find out something, anything, about Kelly's disappearance. Since the Mayor, George's father, worked so closely with Sheriff Tom, he had to know something. "Do you have any leads? Please, anything?"

"Right now I have nothing at all," Grafton said, shaking his head. "I'm going to be meeting with the Sheriff later. We have some things to go over."

"So you're working on it, right? I mean, you have a list of suspects, you have an idea of where she can be-" Mary was cut off by the Mayor putting a hand lightly on her shoulder.

"We're doing everything we possibly can right now," he said politely but firmly, "I told you I'll keep you abreast of everything, and I will. You have my word."

"You promise, she's my best friend." Mary felt an overwhelming panic clutch at her heart, and she started to shake.

"I understand that, and I understand you're upset, but right now I don't have time for this," Grafton was calm, but he was annoyed, and it was beginning to show as he continued to speak to her. "We doing everything that we possibly can. Why don't you just go ahead and enjoy the game"

"Okay," Mary nodded vigorously, trying to hold her emotions in check. "You promise you will let me know?"

"I promise, okay?" He grinned tightly at her. "I give you my word, and my word is law around here."

George walked over to them holding a cup of hot chocolate. He put his arm around Mary.

"Hello Mary," George said with mock enthusiasm. "Hi Dad, what's up?"

"I was just leaving." Mary said with a nervous smile. "Bye."

"Bye Mary," Mayor Grafton said, watching her walk away. "What a pain in the ass she is." He was shaking his head, still annoyed as George stepped over to his side.

"So Dad, you should see all of the girls in this school. A bunch of bitches. It sucks!"

"Yeah, definitely." The Mayor agreed.

Mary found a seat on the bleachers nearby, and began to read more of the spell book while glancing up on occasion to watch the game, which had just started. George walked over to the section of bleachers she was sitting at and sat down next to her. Not being a big fan of George, even though he was a friend of Fred's and the mayor's son, she made an exasperated face and leaned back. 'God, he's never happy unless he's starting some kind of shit with somebody.' Mary thought to herself. 'I'll never understand why Fred hangs out with him.'

"Hi Mary," George said, sitting down.

"Yes? What do you want?" Mary's responded, giving him a dirty look and snapping her book shut.

"Listen, I don't want to be the one to tell you this but, remember when Fred told you we saw the team pass right by us right before kick-off?" George sounded sarcastic, and waited for Mary to nod before continuing. "Well, uh, what he forgot to mention was he saw Mark and that 'sparkle bitch' over there," he nodded toward the cheerleaders, "kissing each other, and they seemed to really, really like it."

Mary felt her throat tighten, saw the wicked smile on George's face and immediately wanted to cry, but held her emotions back, trying not to let him get the better of her during the game. She promised herself he was lying, and that she'd talk to Mark about it later and everything would be fine.

George watched Mary's face change from annoyed at him to a slightly upset frown. Pleased that what he told her produced the reaction he wanted, maybe not as intense as he wanted, he pointed to the book she was holding on her lap.

"Isn't that the book from Lundy's class?" George smiled when he heard her sniffle and saw her eyes turn away from him. "Are you going to go all sociologist and explain how mounting tensions forced a local governor to start screaming 'witch' at every young busty Puritan he had a crush on? Or are you going to go all Wiccan on us and turn Lundy into a toad? Please dear God go for the second one." He said folding his hands in a mock prayer gesture. "You're going to be totally ostracized for the rest of your time here, but kids everywhere are going to be screaming, 'Mary Horowitz' in pure fear. Naw, that sounds way too wordy. 'Mary Horowitz', that sounds more like a nasty old librarian. It's not really the image of terror we're looking for here. I know, shhh, wait, let me say it: Mary Horror." George, thinking that he'd made Mary even more upset with his new nickname, turned to her and smiled.

"Mary Horror," Mary repeated with an evil grin, determined not to show him that what he had said had gotten to her in any way. "It sounds too Christmassy."

"What do you care? You're Jewish, you don't even celebrate Christmas." George laughed.

"We still celebrate Christmas because of my Mom." She replied coldly. Mary turned away and focused on the game, ignoring him completely.

For a few minutes they both sat silently, watching the game, listening to the people around them yell and scream. Mary kept hearing what George had said about Mark cheating on her repeatedly in her head. She was starting to get upset and feared that she couldn't hold it back much longer.

"Y'know, I really like you Mary," George said, speaking up suddenly with a serious look on his face. "Maybe that's why I had to tell you about Mark." He paused, waiting for Mary to say something, anything. "Alright, I'm out of here." He said, abruptly getting up when he saw that she wasn't responding at all. He stepped down from the bleachers and angrily kicked and empty soda can. Mary could only watch him walk away, her eyes slowly filling with tears. She felt as if her life was falling apart, and there was nothing she could do about it, no way to stop it.

*****

Mayor Grafton was still leaning on the bleachers when Sheriff Tom showed up.

"So, did you get the bet down?" Sheriff Tom asked, casually folding his arms, leaning next to the Mayor.

"Yeah I did." Grafton nodded.

"Good." Sheriff Tom grinned and nodded. "What kind of odds are we getting this year?"

"Uh, we got three to one." He said, staring off toward the field where the game was still going on.

"Well, the team's a lot better this year." Sheriff Tom replied.

"Yeah they are. We're gonna make a lot of money on this one." Grafton smiled at the Sheriff, who chuckled and nodded. "It's all good."

*****

After the game, Mary found herself wandering around the school grounds. Too many things were running through her head for her to settle down or even drive home. By the time most of the crowd had left the field, she finally sat down and leaned against the door to the gym. The spell book seemed to call to her. She flipped it open and started reading again. She was learning more and more about the spells, rituals; things she'd never been able to imagine on her own.

Fred had long since finished handing out all of his flyers, and ended up watching the tail-end of the game at the far side of the field. He started to walk back to his car when he saw Mary sitting against the gym door. He felt guilty about not saying anything to her about seeing Mark and 'sparkle girl' and stopped to see if she was okay. He was still debating internally about whether or not he should tell her what he saw.

"Hey," he asked, putting a hand on her shoulder. "Are you okay?"

Mary just shook her head, looking as if she was about to start crying.

"Come sit," she whispered, tapping the space next to her. Fred sat down and she put her head on his shoulder. He felt her shudder, sob.

"My family and I are moving away." He said quietly.

"What?" Mary pulled away and looked at him in shock.

"We can't be in this town anymore. We're going to keep the search going, but it's just too painful for us to be here anymore." He stared off into the night. "It's just too painful."

"What am I gonna do without you?" Mary said tearing up. "You're the only one besides me that seems to care about Kelly."

"You'll be fine," Fred whispered. "Everything will be fine."

Mary settled her head back on his shoulder again, and for a moment the awkwardness she always felt for Fred was gone.

"Is it true, about Mark?" She asked, dreading but needing to hear his answer.

She saw the answer when Fred just put his head down and looked sad. She couldn't hold back anymore and the tears started to fall.

"I'm so sorry I didn't tell you. I feel like such an idiot, but I really just didn't want to cause any problems. There's already too much bad stuff going on." He looked her in the face. "I saw it happen."

"You did!" Mary stammered, pulling away to look him in the face. "Tell me, what happened? What are all the details, tell me everything you saw."

"There really isn't that much. I was at my locker and I saw them together. One minute they were whispering to each other, and then they just started kissing. I'm sorry. I should have told you sooner but, I'm sorry." Fred exhaled loudly and rubbed Mary's arm, trying to comfort her. He put a hand to his forehead and shook his head.

They sat there in silence for a few minutes, than Fred walked Mary to her car. Neither one said more than 'goodbye', the awkwardness having returned. Mary wanted to wait for Mark, and if anything, confront him about what she was told.

The pain was something she'd never felt before, because she'd never been that close to any guy before. He meant everything to her, and now she felt crushed. For a while she cried, then anger started to build up and she wanted to scream.

She opened the spell book, propped it against the steering wheel and started to read it from the beginning again.

'They call me Rebecca, but I know that deep within, I am something else. I am different. Your witch blood flows within, and there is no stopping it.'

Mary got through the first paragraph, but stopped when she heard the gym door slam, breaking her concentration, and allowing the anger and hurt to return.

"Caring for someone, loving someone; it's like handing them a loaded gone and hoping they won't shoot you." She mumbled when she saw Mark emerge from the gym, shoulder pads swinging from one arm and the other holding the backpack that had his uniform in it. He walked to her car as if he hadn't a care in the world.

"Hey, everything warm in there?" He smiled and tapped on the driver's side window, dropping what he carried.

Mary got out of the car. She was angry and sad at the same time, and it was clear by the way her eyes looked that she'd been crying.

"Did I do something wrong?" Mark asked, stepping back from her.

"Obviously you did something wrong!" Mary shouted. "Okay, I heard about what you did!"

"Heard about what?" Mark asked, acting surprised, as if he had no idea what she was talking about.

"About what happened in school today in front of everybody!" She gestured at him with outstretched palms, her face growing red with anger. "Did you think that no one was going to tell me anything? I mean, do you think I was really that stupid?"

"Unless you're talking about the guy that faked tea-bagging me at the end of the game," Mark stepped closer to her and pointed to the football field, "I have no idea what you're talking about!"

"I don't believe you, okay!" Mary started to shout even more loudly than before. "Everyone saw you making out with Kim today in the hallway! You might as well have just put up a sign, 'Yeah, we're fucking each other!'"

Mark moved closer to her and put his hands on her arms, trying to get her to calm down while he tried to think of a way out of the situation before it got any worse.

"What has gotten into you? Seriously! You know I have to act a certain way in front of the crowd." He shouted above Mary, who had turned away and shouted 'Oh God' in disgust. "It's like Mr. Peterson says in Media and Society, sex sells, and I have to sell the fuckin' team!"

"That's bullshit!" She shouted at the top of her lungs. "You don't have to sell anything, okay? I should be more important to you than selling some stupid football team with some stupid cheerleader! I care more about you than that! God I hate you!" Mary's words were so loud, so hateful and angry, that Mark didn't have time to get a word in. She jumped back into her car and slammed the door shut.

"C'mon Mary, stop!" He said, standing next to the car. "C'mon, just stop, seriously!"

Mark tried to say it again, but it was too late to stop Mary. She started the car and slammed her foot on the gas, speeding away from him.

"Fuck!" Mark shouted, punching the air.

The drive home was like a season in hell for Mary. She cried so hard it hurt, so she got angry and smacked the steering wheel over and over again until her hands hurt. She tried turning the radio on to focus her mind on music, but the local DJ was no help.

"This Is DJ Red, and you're listening to 88.7 FM! This next song goes out to all of you going to the Homecoming Dance tomorrow night."

The song that began to play, 'Die in your arms', from a local band, 'Crash Romeo', makes her cry even more, because she and Mark used to listen to it all the time. Her foot has a mind of its own and she speeds up, the spell book slipping off the passenger seat. Absently, she reaches over, lifts it up as the car speeds along, and puts it back on the seat under her purse.

Mary starts to think about everything that's happened to her over the past few months. Moving to Bernardsville, her grandmother dying, her best friend disappearing, reduced to a face on a 'Missing' flyer, and now, how her relationship with her boyfriend has fallen apart.

She wouldn't be going to the Homecoming Dance.

She pulled into the driveway to her house by instinct alone, not even realizing that she'd gotten home. Her mind was so far away from her actions. She just wanted to curl up into a tiny ball and disappear in a corner somewhere.

When it dawned on her that she was actually home, she realized that she'd missed 'family night' because of what had happened at the football field; how she stayed way too long and not even called home. She thought of her mother, and how she just wanted to curl up in her arms so she could make everything feel better.

Her mind goes through what happened when she reached the house; how she saw the bodies, the blood. Her father, reaching out to her with his last breath-

FIVE

Mary's eyes blinked open, and she was momentarily blinded by the brightness of her hospital room. The window, how bright the light from it was, told her it was morning.

She could still hear her father calling out to her.

"Mary." She heard it again, only it wasn't in her flashback of a dream.

Through her blurry vision she could see someone standing next to her hospital bed. The person was shrouded in shadow, and leaning forward, reaching for her with an outstretched hand.

"Mary, honey, you're going to be okay." The figure said.

The sound of the voice she heard caused Mary to jerk herself up in bed, abruptly completely aware of her surroundings. She winced in pain at her own sudden movement, which caused the tube in her arm and the bandage around her stomach to shift. Shockingly, she saw her father standing next to her bed.

He was dressed in a suit and tie, looking no worse for wear, considering she'd seen him bloodied and dying the night before. She must have imagined it, she had to have, because he wouldn't be standing in front of her if he was dead like her mother and younger brother.

'Maybe I'm just going crazy, and nobody's dead, and I imagined it all?' she thought to herself as her father took her hand into his own.

"You're going to be fine Mary. Everything is going to be alright, Daddy's here now." He said, smiling at her.

"Daddy?" Mary felt her face warm up and tears began to fall. "Daddy, how are you here?"

"I took Rooftop to Main Street and it took me here." He winked at her. "It's the same way I travel to work every day, silly girl."

Her father hugged her lightly, then pulled away and stood up straight as Dr. Hess entered the room.

"Well, it's good to see families coming together in times of crisis. How are you feeling Mary?" The doctor stood on the other side of her bed smiling at her.

"Uh, okay now." Mary said, completely confused, but happy to see her father.

"Very good," Dr. Hess said, stepping back out of the room again.

Mary pulled her father's hand to her face and started to cry. He kissed her lightly on the forehead and tried to reassure her that everything was going to be okay.

*****

The next few days were a blur to Mary. Apparently she hadn't been as gravely injured as she'd thought, and before she realized it, she was driving home with her father in his white BMW as if all was right in the world again.

Her mother and brother were waiting outside for them as her father pulled into the driveway. Mary was so excited she couldn't stop smiling. She practically jumped out of the car and hugged her family. Together, they all walked to the house, about to step inside-

All of a sudden, Madam Ruth was there. Mary saw her as if she were standing right in front of her. She pointed to Mary and repeated the warning that had sent a chill up her spine that day on the boardwalk.

"You be careful girl," Madam Ruth shouted, pointing to her. "If you don't get rid of that book, bad things are gonna happen!"

Madam Ruth vanished, and more images flashed in front of Mary. The entire night played out again, and she saw her family dead in her house. They were all bloodied and dead, including her father.

Awareness, she was finally awake, really awake.

Mary was in a lot of pain. She forced her eyes open and sat up in bed with a gasp of pain, and knowing that her father wouldn't be there this time. He wouldn't be there for her ever again in the real world.

Dr. Hess, wearing a lab coat, pushed the curtain around her bed aside and stepped up to her bed. He held a small plastic cup in one hand, and what looked like a couple of pills in the other.

"Hello Mary." He said, coming up close to her. "Did you have another nightmare tonight?"

She simply nodded, her expression going blank.

Mary saw Sheriff Tom across the room, standing against the wall next to the open curtain.

"Well, usually the nurse would give you the pills, but I'll be administering them to you today." He handed Mary her pills and the cup of water.

Mary didn't know what else to do besides take them. Her body was a mass of pain and her head hurt, not just where the bandage was but also from the emotional torment of the nightmare.

"Now, let's see here," Dr. Hess said, lifting up her chart and flipping through it. "Um, we have a police officer here that wants to ask you a couple of questions."

Sheriff Tom seemed cocky, strolling in the room like the captain of a winning football team. He looked at Mary then turned toward the doctor looking uneasy.

"Is she okay?" He nodded toward Mary. "She seems kind of out of it."

"She's fine." Dr. Hess replied. "She's been through a lot. We had to pump her with about 10 ccs of Rebuteral, but that should have worn off by now."

"Mary, my name is Sheriff Thomas Walker, you've probably seen me around town." Sheriff Tom was carrying something, holding it close. Mary saw that it was her spell book and grabbed it from him before he could say another word. Sheriff Tom edged slightly away from her bed and nodded to her. "I found that in your car. I've been working with your Dad on a project for the town. He's a good man." He leaned over the bed, staring directly at her. "Mary, I'd like to ask you a couple of questions about what happened at your house last night."

"Okay," Mary's words were spoken just above a whisper. She knew very well who Sheriff Tom was, and for some reason, unlike George's opinion of him, the Sheriff made her very nervous, nearly scared.

"Do you know who was in your house? Did you get a good look at him?" Sheriff Tom was speaking casually, as if he were asking her what she liked on a burger, and not about her family's murder.

"No," Mary replied softly. "When I came in, it didn't even seem like anyone else was there. Then all of a sudden he dropped out of nowhere like he was a-" She managed to speak more loudly, but couldn't find the words to describe her attacker. Whoever it was reminded her of the nightmare she'd been having about her best friend's disappearance.

"Like what?" Sheriff Tom asked skeptically.

"Like a ghost." Mary said fearfully.

Sheriff Tom stood tall and sighed. He clearly didn't like what he was hearing, but he knew Mary was hurt badly and didn't want to make things worse. He had to force himself to go easy on her questioning.

"Don't you worry Mary," he said, suddenly smiling. He put his hand on her leg, rubbing her knee. "Everything's going to be just fine."

Mary wanted to scream the moment his hand touched her, but she couldn't, she was afraid. Something was wrong, but she couldn't figure it out. She sobbed and started to tear up. Then Dr. Hess was there.

"Mary needs to rest now." He said firmly. Both he and Sheriff Tom looked at each other as if something had gone unsaid but was understood.

"Fair enough," he replied, pulling his hand away from Mary's leg. "Mary, thank you for your time. I'll be by soon to see how you're doing," he tipped his hat at her, then paused to look at the doctor as if he was very annoyed, "Good day Dr. Hess."

Both the Sheriff and the doctor left her alone, and she felt like she could breathe easy for a moment. She could see around the curtain. There was a window into the next room. The two of them were standing there and it looked as if the doctor was arguing with Sheriff Tom. Then Dr. Baxter was there, and she looked like she was yelling too. Both of them were yelling at Sheriff Tom, and suddenly, he and Dr. Hess left the room.

"What in hell is going on?" Mary mumbled to herself. "What could they possibly be fighting about?"

Dr. Baxter walked in. She looked flustered, out of breath, and was holding something behind her back.

"Mary, we're going to get you out of here and take you to a place where you'll be well protected and well cared for.

Everything's going to be alright." She pulled a large syringe from behind her back and added it to her IV tube.

Mary felt the world slowly fade away as the contents of the syringe raced through her system.

*****

Dr. Baxter felt the heavy burden of guilt slam hard on her as she tossed the syringe into the hazardous waste container in Mary's room. The sedative was very strong and had quickly done its work; she was out like a light.

From what she knew of her from their visits, Mary was a truly troubled girl. She needed therapy, and a lot of it, especially with her family gone.

Two strong looked orderlies entered the room and started gathering Mary's things and preparing her for transport. Dr. Baxter nodded a greeting to them and left.

As she walked out of the hospital, she couldn't help but think there was something illegal going on besides Mary getting locked away. She didn't understand why Mayor Grafton so adamantly wanted her put away in the Gravestone Psychiatric hospital. It wasn't a hospital with a great reputation in the medical field, and mostly housed insane criminals, so it really made no sense. She signed what she had to in order for Mary's transfer to go through, knowing that there was no further arguing with anyone about it. Grafton and Sheriff Tom pretty much ran the entire town, so there was no going against them.

SIX

Michael Chadwick was a nervous wreck. As an author his first novel did well, very well, but since then everything he'd written had tanked in the worst way. He'd begun to wonder if he'd ever have a bestseller again, and unfortunately, so did his publisher. She'd called while he was picking up his morning coffee and as soon as he saw the number flash on his phone he knew he was in trouble.

"Michael, I'm telling you, you need to think of something, you need to think of a bestseller." Kristen Reynolds was an ambitious young executive at the publishing company that had been working with Michael. She was pushing harder than usual of late, and it only seemed to make things more difficult for him.

"Nothing's coming to me," he said, his sweaty palm causing him to grip his phone tighter. "It's like I have writer's block or something."

"Well, as your publisher, I'm telling you, you need to find out what's wrong and fix it." She sat back in her chair and gestured with her free hand as if he were standing right there. "Your last two books did nothing in the market. I don't know how long I can keep you on at this rate." There was a knock on her door. "Damn, I gotta go," she said in a rush, "My aunt is here and we're supposed to be having lunch together. I'll get back to you." She didn't wait for a goodbye she just clicked off the phone. "Come in." She called out.

"Ready for lunch?" Dr. Baxter asked, standing in the doorway. She loved spending time with her niece. She was young and always striving for something. It reminded her of her first few years of psychiatry, when she thought she could change the world just by caring.

"Yes, I'm just, well a little stressed." Kristen put her hands over her eyes and shook her head. "I'm dry, I need ideas."

"Did you hear about the family that was murdered in Bernardsville?" Dr. Baxter hadn't spoken to anyone about Mary and her family, and was nearly bursting at the seams by the time she got to Kristen's office.

"No," Kristen squinted at her, confused. "What are you talking about?"

"Everyone is gone," Dr. Baxter made a sweeping gesture with her hands, "except for the daughter, who was promised confidentiality. I can't keep this in anymore, I have to tell someone, and I know I can trust you. The daughter, she's my patient, Mary Horowitz." She felt relieved the moment she mentioned Mary's name. "You have to keep quiet about this, but I'm beside myself with worry. Something's going on besides those murders, but I can't figure out what it is."

"I tell ya what, I have to make a quick phone call, and I'll meet you in the lobby." Kristen wanted to jump out of her seat but settled for smiling at her aunt.

"Okay, I'll see you downstairs then" Dr. Baxter said. "We can talk more over lunch."

"Absolutely!" She said enthusiastically.

As soon as her aunt closed the door, Kristen picked up the phone and called Michael Chadwick back.

"Hey Michael, I've got your bestseller idea." She smiled

"Really?" Michael couldn't help but be doubtful. He'd gone through his entire file of story ideas since he'd arrived home and still couldn't come up with a powerful story idea.

Kristen was in a hurry, but she rattled off enough information for Michael to begin putting a scenario together. Then she told him the town the murders took place in and he nearly jumped out of his skin.

"Bernardsville! That's where my niece Kelly went missing!" His heart was suddenly racing and then he got angry. "They still haven't found her. It's like they stopped looking! I'll get right on this! There has to be some kind of connection!"

He hung up with Kristen and made a pot of coffee. More caffeine would only give him some fuel and remind him of what it was like when he was wired and writing that first bestseller. He flicked on the TV and sure enough, the news was already broadcasting about the murders.

He turned up the volume and sat back, jotting down notes when he saw the reporter come on the screen.

"This is Chuck Marble with News 25. Joining us here is Johnson County Sheriff Tom Walker. Sheriff, what can you tell me

at this point about Mary Horowitz?" The reporter held the mike up to the Sheriff.

"Well, at this time she's being held in protective custody at an undisclosed psychiatric hospital. And uh, Mayor Grafton and I assure everybody that she's going to receive the best treatment possible. Other than that, there's not really much more we can comment on. The investigation is still continuing and we haven't concluded anything."

"Are you able to talk about her mental state or her well being at all?"

"The psychiatrists are going to do many tests on her and I'm sure that probably in a week or so we'll know more. There's not much more I can tell you at this time." The Sheriff had begun to sweat. He didn't like having to answer to anyone, especially on camera.

"So she's not allowed to have any visitors and anything like that?"

Sheriff Tom grinned tightly. "Like I said, there's not much more I can tell you."

"Johnson County Sheriff Tom Walker following up on all leads pertaining to the 'Mary Horror' case and is hard at work on the investigation."

"My ass he is!" Enraged and frustrated, Michael flicked off the TV and rushed into his room. He paced for a minute, then went in his closet and pulled out a suitcase. He didn't think it would take him too long to pack.

*****

The few hours it took for him to drive to Bernardsville from the city allowed him to get his head straight about the entire situation. His niece Kelly had been missing for months. And from what he remembered, Mary Horowitz was a friend of hers. He could swear he saw them both in pictures at Kelly's house.

"Something's going on," he muttered angrily, "something really fucked up."

As he drove into town he tried to remember the name of the 'cop bar' that his sister brought him to when he visited her a few months ago. He couldn't think of the name and it pissed him off, but then he remembered where it was in town and a few minutes later he was walking in, still pissed off but hoping to get a beer, and maybe even run into one of Bernardsville's finest, or maybe even good old Sheriff Tom himself.

After drinking several beers and doing a couple of shots, he went outside to have a cigarette; a vice he'd given up after his first novel made it big, but had since picked up again when his niece went missing and his stories started to flop.

"This is taking too long." He decided to get a room in a motel nearby and stay for a few days. He would have stayed with his sister and her family, but since Kelly's disappearance they had decided to move out of town. Michael didn't want to make things harder for them by telling them what he suspected, at least not until he had some concrete evidence. He concluded that he would spend his days in the motel trying to write, and make sure that his nights were at the bar, where he could find the sheriff or even a deputy and hopefully get some information.

The following night, he got his wish. It was nearing closing time when Sheriff Tom walked in. He ordered a beer and sat at the bar. Michael had already had a few, but his mind was clear enough to walk naturally over to the sheriff.

"Sheriff?" He asked, leaning on the seat next to him.

"Who wants to know?" Sheriff Tom replied, gulping down some of his beer.

"Michael Chadwick."

"What's a Michael Chadwick?" He glanced at him sarcastically and then continued to drink his beer.

"I'm doing a story on the Horowitz case, and I thought you could help me out with some questions I have." Michael tried to sound casual.

"Well ya thought wrong Butch." Sheriff Tom looked away and chugged some more of his beer.

"I guess I should have expected that after seeing all you did for my niece." Michael stared at him, clearly annoyed.

"And who might that be?" He said, squinting at Michael.

"Kelly Slater." He replied, continuing to stare at him.

Sheriff Tom rolled his eyes.

"Look, we're doing the best we can pal. Why don't you just get the fuck out of here?" He shook his head and slammed down his empty glass.

"Oh, you'll be seeing a little bit more of me." Michael chuckled and left.

"That'll be a joy." Sheriff Tom sighed loudly, than gestured to the bartender for another beer.

SEVEN

I woke up in a psychiatric hospital. When they told me they were keeping me there so I was safe and protected, I freaked. They ended up strapping me down and drugging me, trying to convince me it was for my own good. It went on like that for months, and I couldn't tell who I was supposed to be afraid of; a masked killer, or the people in the white lab coats poking me with needles every time I tried to get straight answers about anything. It was crazy, no pun intended.....

Somehow I knew nothing was ever going to change. I'd been committed, permanently, and I didn't even know why. The nurse that was always assigned to me, Cloris, kept me fed on pills that made me weak and confused. I managed to heal from my wounds, but everything else that was done to me made me worse in every other way.

I never saw Dr. Baxter again after she'd in effect 'shanghaied' me with a needle. Dr. Hess made an appearance on occasion, to perform what he called 'exams', but I considered them momentary checks just to make sure the guidelines for me being there and the paperwork needed to keep me there was being followed up on. Hess didn't seem to really care about my well being, and seemed more interested in getting his rocks off with one of the nurses and stealing a bit of Vicodin. For all intents and purposes, he was a worthless jackass that had condemned me to a life in a 'nuthouse'.

I had no contact with the outside world, not even a television. They never even gave me my personal belongings, the items I was brought in with, except for my spell book. They seemed to think that was harmless. Little did they know....

I did find out that Dr. Baxter retired suddenly. Dr. Hess told me. It was one of the few questions I asked that he ever answered, but of course he could have been lying to me, or maybe Baxter couldn't live with the guilt of having me locked up.

I never heard a word about Kelly being found. When I tried to ask about her the only answer I got was a quick shot in the arm and a smile from wonderful Nurse Cloris, 'Nurse Ratchet' was more like it.

"Don't worry about her honey," she'd always said grinning at me. "Just concentrate on getting better yourself."

My spell book was my only true escape. Rebecca and her life became so close to me that at times it was as if I was living her life through the pages of her diary. Lord knows I had no life of my own. I knew every spell in that book, and practiced them as much as I could in my mind.

After two years passed, I really started to wonder why I was still there. There wasn't really any reason. I wasn't sick, though I had lost a ton of weight, and emotionally, well, everyone in my life was gone, dead, and by that time my soul had even sort of 'left the building'. What would keeping me there accomplish for anyone?

*****

Michael Chadwick could find nothing in Bernardsville to help him write his story. He tried to research Kelly's disappearance, but the investigation was still considered ongoing and sealed. He tried to get in touch with Dr. Baxter, the psychiatrist that had Mary committed, but found out that she'd retired and didn't do interviews regarding the case.

He got nowhere, so after a few months he moved back to his apartment. He wrote a children's book that sold enough to pay his bills, but he could never keep Kelly, Mary, and Bernardsville too far away from his thoughts.

Catching a glimpse of the news changed his outlook on all of it, even after nearly two years had passed.

"This is Chuck Marble with News 25 here in Bernardsville. Nearly two years have passed and tourists are still flocking to the house where it all happened. Find out why tonight at 11."

The short commercial gave Michael the shot in the arm he needed in figuring a way to get answers and succeed in writing his book and maybe even solve a couple of mysteries along the way. An idea formed in his head, and he wanted to kick himself for not thinking of it before.

Michael returned to Bernardsville that night and checked in to the same room he'd had before. After unpacking, he headed for the bar, remembering that it was called JC's Pub this time around.

Sitting at the bar, he ordered nonalcoholic beer. He didn't normally drink it, but for his plan to work, he needed to stay as sober as he could for when Sheriff Tom arrived, if he actually showed up.

"Let's hope that useless bastard is greedy too." Michael mumbled over his beer. If the Sheriff didn't show, he vowed to do a few shots before closing just to catch a buzz so he could sleep peacefully without being haunted by Mary and Kelly.

Sure enough, shortly before midnight Sheriff Tom sauntered into the pub. The place had about a dozen customers but he spotted Michael right away.

"What are you doing here Chadwick? I thought I told you not to come around these parts." Sheriff Tom said, coming around to his side. He stood leaning over the seat next to him looking annoyed. "You remember what I told you right?"

Michael slightly closed his eyes, and acted as if he was already close to drunk.

"I'm not here for any trouble. You want a beer?" He said, pointing to the bartender, hoping his slurred words weren't too much of a dead give-away.

"Hm, I guess you're speaking my language after all." Sheriff Tom sat down and the pair started drinking heavily. Michael was still getting the same nonalcoholic beer, but the Sheriff didn't know it and had talked him into doing a couple of shots along the way. For a while, the two of them talked about general things, but then it was as if a switch had been turned on in the Sheriff, and the alcohol had finally hit. All of a sudden he started bragging about the town and how the tourist attraction of the Horowitz house had put them on the map.

"Yeah, this 'Mary Horror' shit has been great for business around here." He laughed and slapped Michael on the back. "And you're never gonna believe it, but the Mayor's own son came up with the name 'Mary Horror' before the murders even happened! He actually used to like that crazy bitch!"

"Wow, that's hilarious!" Michael stammered, wanting to smile, because he'd found the perfect opening. "I wonder where the hell she is these days. Is she even still alive?"

Sheriff Tom started laughing. He slapped the bar and smiled squarely at him. "I know where Mary is." He boasted with a devilish laugh. "I've got a proposition for you."

"If it involves money, I'm in." Michael said, exaggerating his movements, glad he didn't have to be the one to try to negotiate a deal.

"It does," Sheriff Tom said, continuing to laugh, "sure as shit it does."

*****

The morning was dreary, with a light drizzle staining the window Mary stared out. Sometimes she liked to watch the sunrise if she was awake, but that morning, even though there was a dawn, the sun never seemed to rise.

"Good morning Mary." Nurse Cloris walked in smiling. "I'm going to break the rules for you just this once. Before you get your breakfast, you have a visitor."

For a moment Mary's eyes bulged. She wanted to scream at Cloris, wanted to grab her and shake her until she told her who it was. It was the anger, the anger and frustration of being locked up for as long as she had been, and never being able to see anyone, or even go outside.

She struggled to stand, holding tightly onto her spell book, but shook too much and ended up sitting down on her bed. The medication she was given the night before still had too strong of a hold on her for her to be able to walk around yet.

"You won't be needing that," Nurse Cloris said, reaching for Mary's book.

Mary's face suddenly grew fierce, and her arms, though thin and weak, tensed up, fingers in a death grip around the binding.

"Okay, okay," Nurse Cloris backed off, "You can keep it. I'm sure you won't harm anyone with it, it's not like a weapon or anything."

Mary was still too weak to stand.

Nurse Cloris solved the problem by bringing in a wheelchair. She helped Mary get in and strapped her wrists to the armrests. In the meantime, Mary was trying to force herself to be more alert, to wake up completely from the pills without Cloris knowing so she could function when she saw whoever it was that had come to see her.

A visitor, which in itself was more than a surprise for Mary; because she couldn't possibly imagine who it could be.

'Who even knows I'm here?' she wondered.

"Now you have to remember that Dr. Hess can never know about this. You can't tell anyone, okay?" Nurse Cloris said, wheeling her down a long corridor. Mary nodded, paying close attention to where she was. She wanted to know if there was any way she could get out, escape, if an opportunity presented itself for her to somehow make a break for it.

She was brought to the break room for the maintenance staff. It was small, and dark, with only a small window high up on the far wall. There was a long table in the middle of the room. A man wearing a shirt and tie sat there. He was holding a notebook and a pen. There was a cardboard box on the floor next to him that he was staring at when she came in.

"Mary Horowitz, this is Michael Chadwick. He's a famous author, and he's come to see you, to talk to you." The nurse wheeled her close, and looked at Michael. "You have forty minutes before the shift change. You need to be out of here before then."

"Thanks." Michael nodded and handed her a small envelope. Nurse Cloris peeked inside it, and smiled.

"When you're done going through her belongings just leave them there. I'd better go and let you get to work." She said, than left the room.

Mary was staring blankly at the box on the floor. 'Belongings,' she thought to herself. 'Maybe my purse is in is there?' She didn't even acknowledge that Michael was there or that Nurse Cloris had left.

"Hello, I'm Michael." He stood up and held his hand out to her trying to break the ice and get her attention. He saw that her arms were strapped to the chair and shook his head, confused. 'She's clearly out of it, no threat to anyone, especially as thin as she is.' He thought to himself, 'even if she is a murderer, why strap her in like that?' He quickly undid the leather straps on her wrists and took her hand, shaking it. "It's nice to meet you. I'd like to talk to you. I'm not sure if you know me, but I'm doing a story on you, I'm here for you."

Mary didn't know him, though he looked vaguely familiar. She didn't care. He wouldn't help her, wouldn't get her out of there, so there was no reason to talk to him, or even be in the same room with him for that matter. She did want to see what was in that box though, more than anything in the world at the moment. Her purse meant more than she could possibly tell anyone because it held her salvation inside it.

"You were close friends with my niece before she disappeared a couple of years ago. Kelly Slater? Does the name ring a bell?" Michael asked, wondering if she even heard him.

Suddenly Mary felt her heart in her throat. She pictured Kelly's face on the flyer Fred handed to her the night of homecoming.

"Is she alive?" She blurted out with a scratchy voice, than started coughing.

"I don't know." Michael said, getting her a cup of water from a water cooler against the wall behind him. "I'm sorry, she's never been found."

Suddenly there was life in Mary's eyes. He decided to continue on, hoping to take advantage of her sudden alertness.

"I'd like to start with the most basic question." He leaned back in his chair, pen ready. "Why did you do it? Why did you murder your family?"

Mary couldn't believe what she was hearing. She gasped involuntarily, her eyes widening in shock and anger.

"What? What are you saying?" She said, still raspy. "I didn't kill anyone, my family was murdered!"

"No, you murdered your family, everybody knows this." He said, confused as she denied it again and again, clawing at the surface of the table with her hands as if she were reaching for something.

"No, no, no, I saw it!" Mary said, starting to get upset. "I came home from the game, and he was standing over my father. My brother, mother, they were all dead, and then he chased me into the woods. I fell, and he stabbed me, he stabbed me with a cleaver! He stabbed me, he stabbed me!"

Things didn't make sense to Michael, and it seemed like he'd opened a bigger can of worms than he'd planned to. 'I just wanted to get information for my book, maybe find out something about Kelly that might point me in a direction to find her, but now?' he thought, exasperated.

"Mary, you stabbed yourself after murdering your entire family." He said calmly. "It's on record, public knowledge."

"No." she pleaded, holding her head in her hands. "I didn't do that!" She'd begun to doubt herself, envisioning herself hold the cleaver high in the air. Had she gone insane and actually killed her entire family? "No, I didn't do that!"

"Yes, you did. The newscasts, the tourist, the books, everybody knows." He continued on.

"No, that didn't happen! What kind of crazy shit are you saying?" She pulled her hands away and sat up in her wheelchair.

"Everyone knows." He reached down and pulled out a wide envelope and flipped open the clasp. "Here, look at these." The envelope held newspaper clippings, stills, magazine covers and articles; all pertaining to Mary being the murderer of her entire family, referring to her as 'Mary Horror'. Michael started to lay them out on the table in front of Mary. One of them had a headline that read, 'Own Daughter Kills Family In Cold Blood,' there was another that had a photo of Sheriff Tom giving a press conference about the murders.

"Do you see all these? They call you 'Mary Horror'. Everything in front of you tells the story of how Mary Horror murdered her whole family the night of the homecoming game. Your house has even become a tourist attraction! How can you not know about any of this?"

"No," Mary continued to scream. "Nobody ever said anything to me! Why didn't they ever tell me? I didn't do this! I don't know anything about it! I've been here since that night! They said I would be safe here! They told me I needed to be protected! I haven't even had access to a TV or radio! Not even my belongings! Nothing!" She quickly scrambled to the floor and pushed over the box that Nurse Cloris referred to as her belongings. Everything she had with her that night spilled onto the floor. She saw her car keys, her brush, and a knife her father gave her to carry in her purse. For a second her heart soared! Her salvation was there, just as she'd hoped it would be. Without thinking twice she grabbed the pocketknife and then painstakingly scrambled to get back into her chair.

The spell book seemed to call to her then, warming in her hands. All the while, Mary continued to scream her denial in the murder of her family. "You're lying! You're a crazy fucking liar!" She shouted at the top of her lungs. "I never killed anybody!"

Michael couldn't understand any of it. Mary seemed genuinely ignorant to everything he'd said. Granted, she could be totally insane, but he doubted that seeing her and her reactions right in front of her. 'What the hell is going on?' he wondered to himself. 'This doesn't make any sense'.

The door flung open and slammed against the wall. Nurse Cloris pounced into the room, grabbed Mary and quickly secured her back in her chair, making sure that the bands on her wrists were a notch tighter than before, just to add a little pain to insure she'd never try anything crazy like that again.

"That's enough!" The nurse shouted at her. "Quiet down or I'll sedate you right now!"

"That's not what happened. What he's saying, showing me, nothing happened like that!" She turned and shouted in Nurse Cloris' face, pointing to the papers still on the table, struggling to stay free. "This did not happen that way! Why does everyone think I killed my own family? I didn't do it!"

"I thought you said you were going to be easy with the questions and keep things calm! Not scare the shit out of her!" Nurse Cloris yelled at Michael. "How could you let her get this way you fucking moron?"

"What the hell is going on here? I only asked her one question and it spiraled into this. It wasn't my intention to get her this way." Michael stood up and shouted to the nurse. "I had no idea that she knew nothing about what really happened, and I'm starting to believe her! Why doesn't she know about any of this?" Michael fanned his hand over all the papers he had on the table. "Why has she been so isolated?"

"You see the way she's acting!" Nurse Cloris barked, "She was this way anytime someone tried to question her. She'd go nuts when law enforcement tried to get information out of her. That's why she's here!" She spun the wheelchair around and started pushing Mary away.

"Mary, I'm sorry! I was just trying to get to the real story." He called out as she was wheeled away. "I'm just trying to help you."

Mary was wheeled out in to the hall and Michael could do nothing but watch it happen.

"Now Mary, you cannot tell Dr. Hess about any of this, understand?" Nurse Cloris said in a threatening manner. "Let's get you calmed down. Let's get you some medication."

"This is unbelievable!" He put everything together, all the papers, and left through the back door of the hospital, ignoring the nurses that were smoking near the door when some of them recognized him.

He knew it wasn't over. There were too many things screwed up in his head about the entire situation now to be left alone, and if it was that way with Mary, he didn't want to think about what could have possibly happened to his niece.

"I've got to get to the bottom of this." He said, starting up his car. "Too much doesn't make sense."

*****

Mary felt the medication Nurse Cloris gave her starting to kick in, but it wasn't half as bad as it used to be.

"I must be getting used to it." She concluded. "Or maybe I'm just too pissed off for it to knock me out right now."

Mary held the spell book close, and slid the knife out from under her gown. She was sitting on her bed, still in utter disbelief of what she saw in the newspaper and other clipping Chadwick showed her. She held her face in her hands, covering her eyes. She didn't know if it was the medication or if she was having a flashback of actual events. She imagined herself holding the meat cleaver the night her family died. She imagined herself swinging it at her family one after another until they were all dead. Finally, she envisioned herself running through the woods, stabbing herself and collapsing in the dirt, screaming.

"Did I do it?" She said, crying with the utter confusion and doubt. It was overwhelming and horrifying at the same time.

"If I did, I didn't know it, wasn't aware of it." She mumbled. "They had no right to do this to me, to lock me away like this! I'll never get out of here!" Anger flared and her eyes narrowed, staring at the spell book.

She grabbed the book and began flipping through the pages until she found the one she was looking for. She remembered asking her grandmother if the spells worked, and could hear her reply as if she were standing next to her.

"They do, but you have to practice." She said. "It must be as if you and the book are one."

"Oh, we're one alright!" She whispered to herself, knowing how close she was to the book, how every word inside it seemed etched in her soul.

She missed her grandmother so much, and knew that had she not died none of this would have ever come to be. But her gift had saved her regardless.

"I can use what she handed down to me to free myself and have my revenge on all of them." She said with a look of grim determination, and a plan forming quickly in her head. "I've had so much time to practice. I have the will, the utter desire, to make it happen. If I fail, at least I tried, and even failure means freedom from this hell."

The spell book was opened to the page she desired. On it there was a sketch of a non-gendered person, with a specific area marked alongside the written spell. Mary stared at it, attempting to stay calm, strong. She carefully lifted the knife from where she'd put it on the bed and stood up, taking deep breaths.

Holding the book in one hand and the knife in the other, she began to recite the spell.

"Call me Mary Horror by name and I will rise from the witches' blood I came."

With a quick powerful movement, Mary stabbed herself in the chest, gasping as the blade cut deeply into her. She sucked in a deep breath and recited the words again, slowly pulling the knife free.

"Call me Mary Horror by name and I will rise from the witches' blood I came!" She shouted, and stabbed herself once more.

She screamed in pain and had to steady herself against the bed.

"Call me Mary Horror by names and I will rise from the witches' blood I came!" She stabbed herself a final time, and sucked in a rasping wet sounding breath. The spell book dropped from her hand, and she'd begun to feel woozy. It took the last bit of strength she had, but she succeeded in pulling the knife back out of her chest.

Mary let the blade fall to the floor, feeling the warmth of her own blood rapidly covering her abdomen. She pressed both of her hands into it, and smeared the blood on the wall, drawing the symbol her ancestor Rebecca had painted on the cover of the spell book. It was the final act of the ritual, and Mary was glad, because she could no longer stay on her feet. A sigh escaped her lips as she collapsed on the floor in front of her bed in a heap, a peaceful expression on her face as she took her last weak breath of air.

*****

Nurse Cloris was making her rounds when she heard the scream, Mary's scream. The nurse ran down the long dimly lit corridor to Mary's room, pushing through the door to find her lying, unmoving on the floor, covered in blood, with some of it smeared on the wall.

Nurse Cloris screamed herself, like she'd never screamed before. She screamed until she ran out of breath.

EIGHT

Michael got back to his room at the motel after his trip to see Mary and started to write down everything he knew from his visit with her. He wanted to commit all the stray thoughts he had to paper before he forgot any of them. When he was satisfied that's he'd filled enough pages with memories, ideas, and even speculation, he sat back to take a break with a beer from the small refrigerator in his room and the news.

"What the fuck is going on in this town?" He said aloud, chugging his beer. "Nothing makes any sense. We have a girl that's supposed to be a murderer, only she didn't even know it herself, and yet, she's locked up in an asylum. My niece, who was her best friend, vanished never to be seen or heard from again, and we have the wonderful Sheriff Tom Walker, who exchanged Mary's location with me for a cut of any advance I get from writing a book about her and the murders she committed." He squeezed the beer can after taking the last sip. "But, of course she doesn't really know she did it, insisting that someone was there at her house that night dressed in black. Yeah, sure, I'm going to be able to figure this out." He said, exasperated, flopping down on his bed. "If I keep this up I'll end up in the same hospital Mary's locked up in."

*****

"A week after Mary Horror's death, the events here are in full swing in Bernardsville, New Jersey, the second anniversary of the now famous Horowitz murders. The town has gone all out, giving tourist what they want. We'll be here throughout the night to give you more on the events as they happen. This is Chuck Marble, News 25."

Michael Chadwick, still in the motel room, turned the volume of the TV down and cursed to himself when he saw an ad come on the screen from Mayor Grafton, asking for more votes in the coming election.

"His hand is in the pot from all of this 'Mary Horror' garbage." Michael shook his head, the feeling of guilt still weighing heavy on him regarding Mary's death by her own hand.

Another commercial flashed on the screen. He couldn't believe what he was seeing. It was a man in a hockey mask, wearing a black cape.

"It's Mary Horror Night!" The masked man said with a bad Bela Lugosi accent. "Come on down to Olcott Square this Tuesday! We have fake cleavers, spell books, Mary Horror T-shirts and more!" He threw a sample of each item at the screen as he called out what they were. It was like a twisted version of an old 'Crazy Eddies' Commercial. "Walk the trail of horror and see where Mary killed her family!" The man said, raising his mask and laughing ghoulishly. He spouted off a phone number and web address.

Michael shut the TV off before another one came on, disgusted with Bernardsville's new version of 'Halloween'.

*****

The Holy Cross Cemetery was the oldest graveyard in the county. Some of the graves, among the sea of headstones dated back well over a hundred years. Andy Riley, and Paul Rodgers, part-time grave diggers from the coroner's office didn't really care about any of that. Driving through the old rusty gates in a pick-up truck littered with trash from Andy's frequent junk food binges, they just knew it was late, and they wanted to do their job and get out of there as soon as they could.

DJ Red, the announcer on the radio broke the silence as Paul pulled the truck over at the desired location in the rear of the cemetery.

"Tonight, tonight, tonight! It's Mary Horror Night! Come on down to Olcott Square and visit me, DJ Red for your free Mary Horror t-shirt!"

Andy shut the radio off, angrily smacking the dashboard.

"Fuckin' hell, man, not again! This shit is getting' crazier and crazier every year!" Andy looked at Paul, who was also annoyed. "Last year we had to deal with those Salem Witch people trying to raise the family from the grave and now this!"

"And the year before, remember it was the fuckin' TV cameras everywhere we went." Paul agreed. "This town has turned into a damn circus!"

"I remember it, I remember it fuckin' well!" Andy complained. "I'm sick of this! I've had it with all this shit here, I've fuckin' had it!"

They were quiet for a few minutes, and it looked like Paul was sitting behind the wheel deep in thought.

"Hey Andy, what are we going to get to eat after we bury this one?" He tilted his head to the side, rubbed his scruffy stubble and turned to look at Andy.

"I don't give a fuck what we're gonna eat Paul, pizza, Chinese, who gives a shit? Have you seen the size of me lately? I'm fat as fuck! I'll eat at whatever's open, alright? Let's just get this done so we can get out of here."

Andy struggled to twist around in the truck; out of breath by the time he was able to open the door and swing his legs out.

"This truck is so fucking high, I'm gonna pull my fuckin' nuts out one of these times." Andy fumed, climbing out of the truck.

"Oh, I think I just did!" Paul said, crouching over after getting out.

"Yeah, you probably just did, you pulled your nuts out, and I'm not readjusting them for you." He started to walk toward the bed of the truck.

"You don't have to." Paul reassured him, shaking his head.

"I'm not, not again. I did it that one time, and that one time made me think about everything that is wrong with my life so I'm not doing it again." Andy sputtered his words out so fast he was out of breath when he grabbed the tailgate and flipped it down.

"You don't have to. I'll call a masseuse, Miranda, she's lovely at what she does." Paul waved him off, wanting it to end there.

"You know you want Carlos," Andy said, dead serious. He put a hand on Paul's shoulder. "Stop lying to yourself."

"He's good at what he does, but Miranda-"

"Now where the fuck do you think we're gonna eat, huh?" Andy blurted out, reaching for the body bag in the back of the truck.

"You know where we should go?" Paul pointed at Andy as if he just found the answer to hunger in the world. "JC's Pub. Remember, it's their anniversary? They'll be open late too because of the whole 'Mary Horror' thing."

"Whatever, I guess." He slid the body off the truck.

"They've got everything you want." He lifted one end of the body while Andy grabbed the other. "I've got a really good feeling about that, we should go there."

The pair carried the body slowly toward a hole already dug near the edge of the cemetery, in the woods. They lowered the body into the hole and Paul ran back to the truck for a couple of shovels.

"Paul, you know who's in there, right?" Andy asked when he returned. Paul shook his head. "It's Mary Horror."

"Oh Christ!" Paul jumped back a step, looking down into the hole fearfully.

"I've got the weapon." Andy boasted. "I've got the cleaver in the back of the truck."

"What the hell do you have that for?" Paul looked disgusted.

"Protection. We're in a graveyard at night. Have you seen the film, 'Night of the Living Dead'?" Andy said it as if he were trying to scare Paul.

"Oh c'mon." Paul laughed and the two began to shovel dirt over Mary's body.

"You know," Andy said after a while, looking up from his work. "There's something about burying somebody that makes me even hungrier than I usually am."

Paul stopped shoveling and looked at him. "Are you serious?"

"Yeah, I just want something juicy, like a big juicy cheeseburger, Paul." He smiled, sounding as if he were talking about a woman and not a meal.

"Yeah, with mushrooms and onions," he smiled too, then turned and continued to put more dirt on the body.

Andy rushed through the rest of the shoveling, fueled by his desire for food. He and Paul were done covering the body a few minutes later.

"C'mon Paul, let's get the fuck out of here already." He said, handing Paul his shovel. "God it's fuckin' freezing out her now."

"Yeah, it did get real cold all of a sudden." Paul swung the driver's side door open.

"God damn, you pull your balls just as bad getting in as you do getting out!" Andy complained, climbing back into the truck.

"Well, I already did, so I'm not doing that again." Paul said, and he took it slow getting back in.

"Put the heat on in this shit, it's freezing." Andy pulled a wool hat on his head. "Hey, y'know we didn't even bury her right."

"We didn't?" Paul was confused. "What do you mean?"

"No, we buried her in a shallow grave, it wasn't done right." Andy shook his head. "There isn't even a headstone."

"Well I'm not sticking around to finish, we'll have to come back tomorrow or something to finish." Paul said, tying a scarf around his throat. He was suddenly freezing.

"I'm hungry and I don't give a shit." Andy laughed, "And I've got plans for you this evening."

"What?" Paul looked perplexed.

"You know what I said." Andy slipped on a pair of gloves, surprised that it had gotten so cold he could see his own breath.

"Oh yeah, the Pub you mean?"

"Yeah." Andy confirmed.

"Y'know, it's funny how there's never anything in here to eat, no snacks, not even a bag of chips or anything." Paul also pulled on a wool cap. "I could really use one right now."

"Hey, you know me, if I bring it in the truck I eat it in the truck." He smirked. "There's never any leftovers."

*****

Awareness. That was first.

Then there was heat, warmth all over her, as if she were lying in a tanning bed.

Then there was the itching. Her skin began to itch all over. It was an odd sensation because she still hadn't been able to move her body. It would have been maddening if she wasn't already slightly insane.

She could barely feel herself until her fingers twitched.

The suffocating feeling of being trapped in a plastic body bag didn't frighten her. She knew she was underground, packed in dirt, but it didn't matter.

Mary was back.

Mary knew she was alive again, or at least as close to being alive as her spell allowed. 'The spell worked!' she thought, amazed. The darkness, and the scent of the plastic body bag was overwhelming. So was the truth. She knew the truth about what happened to her. She'd found that out the second she died.

'I didn't kill my family,' she thought to herself with certainty. 'But I'm going to find out who did, and they're going to pay for it!'

There was no time to mourn a life lost, just a reason for revenge.

The dirt wasn't packed tightly around her. Though it took a lot of physical strength, she was able to move. It was like swimming in molasses, but she was able to move her arms, pressing her hands against the constricting bag she'd been sealed inside. Her nails, jagged and unkept due to her time in the asylum dug into the thick plastic, and with her new strength, tore right through it.

Mary sat up underground, freeing herself from the confinement of the bag simultaneously. She kept her mouth and eyes closed, got her feet under her and kicked up from the harder ground under her.

Pushing her arms down she was able to move higher. She reached up, and one hand broke through the ground, sprouting from the loose dirt like a black rose growing in the moonlight. She felt cold air on her fingertips, and anxiously dug herself out.

When she was finally free of her shallow grave, she stood motionless for a moment, gazing at the moon and how the clouds were swirling around it. Suddenly, she wore a smile of utter satisfaction.

Dirt clung to her everywhere. She screamed in the night, her body shaking itself free of the dirt so quickly she was a blur in the starlight. The voices of the men who had buried her echoed in the distance. She followed the sound and found them getting into their truck.

The meat cleaver.

It was in the back of the truck. She could sense it lying there.

People said she murdered her family with it. They lied. All the more reason for her to possess it. All the more reason to use it.

*****

The truck was running but it hadn't warmed up enough yet for the heat to work. Paul and Andy sat inside bundled up. There was a loud crashing sound over their heads. Something had hit the roof of the truck.

"Paul, what the fuck was that?" Andy jumped, panic-stricken.

"Whatever," Paul said dismissively. "Let's just get the fuck out of here already."

As Paul grabbed the gear-shifter there was another loud banging sound.

"We'd better see what the fuck it is." Andy said, opening the door and letting himself slide out of the truck. Paul followed suit, muttering curses.

"Oh shit!" Paul shouted looking at the roof of the truck.

"What the fuck!" Andy echoed.

Standing on the roof of the truck, cleaver in hand and dressed in the gown she was to wear at the Homecoming Dance, was Mary Horror. She looked at them both and smiled wickedly, the dark red of her lips a deep contrast to her pale grayish skin. Not needing any further prompting, the pair ran off screaming, each going in a different direction.

*****

A fence had been built around the Horowitz house since the murders, when it became a tourist attraction. Sheriff Tom was at the front gate, making sure the lock was secure. Mayor Grafton was there with him.

"The gates locked." Sheriff Tom said approaching the Mayor. "I don't want any cars going in with that 'Trail of Horrors' thing going on. I have to go meet those dumb fucks tonight and make sure that she gets in the ground. So there aren't any problems."

"Well, I still haven't gotten the call yet," Mayor Grafton said, puffing on a thick cigar, "but we're gonna hit the jackpot tonight in sales!"

"Well, he's still got his own key right, because this one is staying right here in my pocket." Sheriff Tom tapped his shirt pocket.

"A key? Yeah, he's got a key. I can't be waiting here all night for a pick-up. I've got to go sell crap to the out-of-towners. Hell, then I've got to go preside over the memorial service. It's a busy night." The Mayor's phone rang. "Hold on, this is probably him now." He pulled the phone from his jacket pocket. "Grafton here." He nodded affirmation to the Sheriff, and started laughing as he continued to speak to the caller. "Yeah, you heard right. The stupid bitch killed herself a few days ago. Oh hell, it's not a problem for me, no. Look, I left your money on the kitchen counter. I think next week's cut is gonna be triple considering our little festivities tonight."

"I'm going to see the boys, and make sure everything is going alright. I'll see you in town later on tonight." Sheriff Tom tipped his hat to the Mayor, who nodded and kept on talking. "I can't trust them to do anything alone, the fuck-ups." The Sheriff muttered to himself as he got in his patrol car.

It didn't take the Sheriff long to reach the cemetery. He had the lights on the car flashing and sped through traffic like he was chasing someone. No one ever questioned him no matter what was going on.

The graveyard was dark. He wondered about that, because there were lights around the perimeter that were timed to go on at sunset. "I'd better have that checked out in the morning." He surmised.

Then he saw Andy running and didn't know whether to laugh or yell at him. Andy was big, and he was wearing an orange insulated suit. Running as he was, he resembled an enormous pumpkin. He pulled the car over to the side and got out.

"Hey, what's the problem? I was just coming down to see you guys." He said as Andy ran toward him. He was panting like a race horse and pale as a ghost.

"She's alive Sheriff Tom, she's alive!" He gasped.

"What the hell are you talking about," the Sheriff said shaking his head in disbelief. "Have you and Paul been at that marijuana again? You know, I don't have time for any of your bullshit!"

"No, Mary Horror, she's alive! I'll show you!" Andy persisted, still gasping for breath after running as he did.

"Oh, I've got to see this." He said sarcastically, jerking his thumb at the car. "C'mon, get in!"

"I'm not kidding Sheriff Tom, she's fuckin' alive!" Andy pleaded. "I saw her with that cleaver you sold me. She must have taken it out of the truck somehow. You better get your gun out, she looks pissed!"

Sheriff Tom slammed on the brakes and angrily looked at Andy.

"If you tell anyone about that cleaver I'll charge you with grand theft and have you sent to prison!" He threatened. "You got me?"

Andy simply nodded fearfully, finally catching his breath.

*****

Paul ran as fast as he could. He could hear Mary close behind. She was making some sort of growling noise. In the distance he saw the workshop for the cemetery. They hadn't closed the bay door earlier, so he made a dash for it.

The lights were still on inside. When Paul got there he searched for a place to hide, a place to get away from a woman that should be dead; a woman he helped bury only moments ago. He spotted an old table and ducked under it, closing his eyes and trying to breathe quietly.

It didn't matter. Mary heard him.

She saw him, plain as day, crouched under the table. He helped bury her. She felt rage build within her and swung the cleaver at the table-top, the blade slamming right through it and into Paul's skull. He didn't even have the chance to scream, didn't even know his end was coming.

Mary laughed as she pulled the cleaver free. She stared at it, eyes widening at how the thick dark red blood dripped from it. She heard a siren in the distance, and turned to see a patrol car coming toward the building.

"There she is!" Andy shouted, pointing at Mary as she ran out into the open. "I told you she's alive!"

"Are you sure that isn't just some punk kid out here trying to scare you guys?" Sheriff Tom asked.

"That's no punk kid, that's her!" Andy shouted, going pale again.

"Stay here," the Sheriff shut off the lights and siren and got out of the car. He pulled his gun and started slowly walking toward the building.

She seemed to appear out of nowhere, standing right in front of him holding the cleaver up as if she was going to swing it at him.

"Mary?" He squinted in the dim light to make sure he wasn't imagining things, and then knew it was her just by the smile on her face. He felt sweat suddenly on his forehead, eyes bulging at the dead woman coming at him. "Stop right there," she continued toward him, "I said stop! Stop or I'll shoot!"

When Mary kept coming he fired, hitting her squarely in the shoulder of the arm that carried the cleaver. Mary paused for a second, the force of the bullet shaking her, but continued on. Sheriff Tom fired again, hitting her in the other shoulder, but that didn't even slow her down.

Mary dropped the cleaver and grabbed Sheriff Tom by the throat. He shouted but she only smiled and pulled his face toward her own. Sheriff Tom couldn't break her grip and could only scream as she bit him, her teeth ripping into his left eye. There was unbelievable agony as he felt his eye being torn out of its socket, blood dripping down his face. When she shoved him away a second later all he could do was crumble to the ground in agony.

Mary laughed and spit his eye out so that it landed directly in front of him. She wiped the blood off her mouth, picked the cleaver up and walked away.

Andy couldn't see clearly enough to know what happened to Sheriff Tom. He hoped he was right and it was only some kid playing a prank, but the woman he saw on the roof of the truck looked exactly like he remembered Mary. He heard leaves crunching and thought it might be the Sheriff coming back or maybe even Paul finally showing up. He twisted toward the driver's side door, which was still open, and screamed when he saw Mary getting in, brandishing the meat cleaver.

Mary slammed the cleaver into Andy's head, but didn't stop there. She felt a rush of excitement and continued to swing the blade at Andy, cutting into him all over his body more than a dozen times. When the interior of the patrol car was virtually covered in blood, and even the inside of the windshield dripped crimson she got out and rapidly headed toward the gates of the graveyard.

On the way out she came to a telephone pole with a poster on it advertising 'Mary Horror' night. The memorial service was listed and there was a picture of Mayor Grafton on it. She crumpled it up and quickened her pace into town.

NINE

People crowded the streets in Bernardsville. Mayor Grafton was at a vending table selling 'Mary Horror' T-shirts to dozens of people lined up. There was a lot of cash changing hands there and he was a very happy man.

The movie theater marquee had "Mary Horror Night" in bright red letters that looked like they were dripping blood across it. The theater was running old Chiller Theater movies around the clock and was packed. Inside, George, the Mayor's son sat next to Kim Fines.

"I love how they play all the old horror movies on the night of the anniversary." Kim said, wincing at the bloody action she saw on the screen.

"Yeah, my Dad goes all out." He boasted, munching on popcorn. "Mary Horror, he tells the press, was his genius, but it was really me! I made up the name the night Mary killed everyone and he swiped it from me. Hey, I've got a question for you."

"Okay," Kim nodded.

"Do you still talk to that low-life deadbeat of an ex-boyfriend of yours?" He said continuing to munch.

"Um, you mean Mark?" She said, looking momentarily uncomfortable.

"Yeah, that crack-head still owes me forty bucks," he complained.

"Not really, I haven't seen him." She grinned at George. "Ever since he lost Mary, he's been kind of distant. I don't even know why he cared about her. She kind of freaked me out." She rolled her eyes and sat deeper in her chair.

"Yeah, Mary, what a scary bitch she was." He muttered after jumping at another bloody murder flashing on the screen.

Kim's phone went off. She slipped it out of her pocket, then as something flashed across the screen of the movie, her arm jerked suddenly and she dropped it.

"Shit!' She said, trying to unsuccessfully to pick it up. "Hey, George," she nudged him. "Can you get my phone for me? I dropped it."

"Who was it, Mark?" he said sarcastically. "Okay, but I better not miss anything good." He crouching down, sweeping his hands around to find it. He didn't see Mary, who was suddenly sitting directly behind him.

George found the phone and handed it off to Kim. Mary leaned forward, puckered up and made a kissing sound right in George's ear. Annoyed, George turned around, than nearly fell out of his seat when he saw that it was Mary behind him.

"Holy shit!" George's eye bugged out. "You're supposed to be dead!"

Mary stood up and lifted the cleaver high in the air, ready to swing it at George. She saw the panic in his face and smiled. 'He was such a bastard to me.' She thought to herself. 'And now he's with that little sparkle bitch!'

Kim saw Mary and screamed too. The people sitting around them were in a panic at the sight of Mary, frantically trying to rush out of the theater, shouting and screaming.

George grabbed Kim and ran down the aisle they were in, trying to reach the rear exit. Kim pulled away and ducked into another row of seats. George kept going, and Mary followed him, never too far away.

"Mary, what are you doing, stop!" George shouted, backpedaling, trying to reach the exit that was only a short distance away.

George's terror just added to fuel to Mary's rage. She thrust her hand out and clutched at George's throat. Grabbing him and lifting him off the ground. She held him in the air as the theater emptied, laughing at his gasps. She flipped the cleaver over in her hand so that she held it blade-side up and plunged it into George's abdomen right under his ribs. Blood poured out of his mouth as Mary let go and he fell, sinking further on the cleaver until Mary flung him away.

Kim was racing down an aisle, heading right for the exit. Mary saw her struggling to run in her heels and laughed. She followed her, keeping a distance just to see Kim struggle. She felt satisfaction in watching her cry.

Kim made it outside, screaming. She ran around the back of the building and through the side alley, trying to make it to the street.

Mayor Grafton had stepped away from the vending table to get some coffee from the café next to the theater. He was glad to see a line of people were waiting to get tickets to the next show while he thumbed through a stack of ten's and twenty's.

"This is gonna be a great week for my bank account!" he said aloud, strapping the cash together with a rubber band and stashing it in his pocket.

Suddenly he heard screaming, a woman screaming. For a moment he thought it might have been from the theater, but it sounded as if it was coming from the ally he had just passed. Mayor Grafton back stepped and turned into the alley, hoping it was just a couple of kids messing around and trying to scare people.

Kim, still screaming, slammed right into him.

"Mayor Grafton!" she yelled, looking up at him. "Mayor Grafton, she's back! Run! She's right behind me!"

"Who's back," Grafton asked, unsuccessfully trying to hold onto her to find out. Kim pulled away and kept on running, tears streaming down her face.

The Mayor turned back toward the alley and was immediately confronted by Mary.

"Mary," Grafton stuttered, walking backwards into the alley. He was momentarily mesmerized by the glint of light on the cleaver she carried, and noticed the thick blood dripping from the tip of it. "Mary, you're dead, we buried you! What are you!" he shouted, cringing at the sight of her gray skin and brittle looking hair. He struggled to compose himself and searched his mind for a way to stop her from swinging her notorious, yet fictitious weapon at him.

'I'm Karma on two legs, bastard!' Mary vehemently thought to herself.

"Mary, you're famous. You're famous, I made you famous! All these people are here for you, they love you!" He was so afraid his bladder let loose and he felt his own piss running down his legs.

A young couple was walking up the alley behind them. They were holding each other close and kissing. The moment they saw Mary and the Mayor they both screamed and ran back the other way. Grafton saw them out of the corner of his eye, and in that moment of distraction, stumbled over some trash from a nearby dumpster and fell on his back.

'You just missed seeing your son,' Mary thought with a smile, 'for the last time!' The utter pleasure she felt sent a chill up her spine and she laughed as she swung the cleaver at his legs. Mary hacked and hacked at the limbs, while Grafton screamed a high pitch sound comparable to the shriek of a teenage girl, until they were little more than bloody sections of meat. Blood covered the Mayor, seeping out of the stumps all over the alley.

Mary walked out of the alley and stood, illuminated by the light of a street lamp. She continued to laugh and the people milling about noticed she was standing there and began to run, some of them screaming. She saw children carrying plastic copies of her cleaver and smiled and they ran off, terrified at the sight of her.

Satisfied that she had tied up two more loose ends and made a lasting impression on the town and its people, Mary contemplated making a few more stops before finally going home.

*****

The pain Sheriff Tom felt was more intense than anything he'd ever felt before, even when he was shot while in the military. His face was numb around his eye, but the bleeding had stopped. He struggled to get to his feet, dizzy and unsteady, finding triumph in merely getting to his hands and knees.

He thought about Mary, and remembered the spell book that he'd found in her car. If what he suspected was true, and the whole idea of it would have struck him as insane had he not seen her himself, she was a witch, returned from the dead seeking revenge. Which meant she would be after everyone that crossed her, including the Mayor, Dr. Hess, Dr. Baxter, even her own-" Sheriff Tom's thoughts cut off as he fell back on the ground, unconscious again.

*****

Ever since Dr. Baxter had retired she found that she simply wanted to be referred to as 'Connie'. It made her feel more normal. After the whole situation with the Horowitz family, and how she had made a poor judgment call by telling her niece about it, whom she hadn't spoken to since, she needed to feel normal. The guilt for having Mary Horowitz signed over to the state as insane, knowing she wasn't, was overwhelming, and she vowed to never again practice in her field after committing such an injustice to an innocent girl. Living in Bernardsville was difficult too, because she had Mayor Grafton and Sheriff Tom to contend with.

Never married and with no children of her own, she adopted a mixed breed medium sized dog that she called 'Smoochie'. They were inseparable. She found that walking Smoochie was therapy of sorts, because of the peace and quiet.

On 'Mary Horror Night', Connie took Smoochie out for his normal evening walk and everything seemed quite normal, though it was a bit chillier than she'd expected.

They reached a nearby park where the dog liked to run a little at night and chase squirrels if he saw any, which gave Connie a few minutes to admire the night sky and relax.

When she saw Mary Horowitz, or Mary Horror, as she'd been renamed, coming at her, Connie's mind went blank. She stood there in the park, paralyzed by the sight of the young woman she thought dead; the same young woman that she had wronged.

Mary grinned when she saw Dr. Baxter.

'I don't even have to go to her house now.' She thought, smiling.

It was over for Connie is seconds. Mary leaped high into the air and landed right on her. She was flat on the ground and nearly unconscious when the cleaver found its mark in her throat. The blood poured out of the wound and Mary continued to hack at her.

Dr. Connie Baxter felt pain initially, but as she bled out there was a sense of relief, and her only regret as her life ended, was not having someone to take care of Smoochie for her. The dog had seen Connie attacked, running over to her side as she fell. A Baxter bled out; Smoochie rolled over and played dead at her side.

*****

Dr. Hess caught the tail end of the news while checking over paperwork at the asylum and had to sit down for a moment, too shocked to remain standing. 'How can this be?' he muttered, taking a deep breath and standing. He left his office and ran down the hall to the Rec Room where he knew Nurse Cloris was working.

"Cloris, come with me," he said grabbed her arm and pulling her out of the room. "There's something you have to see."

"What? Wait a minute," she protested, "what's going on?"

"You'll see." He said, pulling her into his office. He sat down on the small couch with her and pointed to the TV. "They're having 'Special Reports' about it every few minutes, so just watch."

Sure enough, a scene directly outside the movie theater in Bernardsville flashed on the screen, and the local news anchor began his latest report.

"This is Chuck Marble reporting for News 25 here in Bernardsville. Despite assurances from Sheriff's Deputies, more and more rumors have begun flowing about tonight's attacks, one of which has left the towns' beloved Mayor, Joseph Grafton dead in the alley adjacent to the Bernardsville Theater. One of said rumors proclaim that tonight's brutal slayings are the work of 'Mary Horror', the local legendary murderess that still brings a steady stream of tourist to the area." Marble lowered his head, pausing to hold his ear while another report was being read to him through is earpiece.

"Another one?" Marble's eyes widened. "We've just confirmed from the Sheriff's Department that another murder has occurred. A retired local Psychiatrist, Dr. Connie Baxter, has been found murdered near her home. The police have no leads but consider her death to be related to the others that have already occurred. We also have reports of several actual sightings of 'Mary Horror'. The Sheriff's Department would like anyone with information regarding tonight's incidents to call the tip-line flashing across the bottom of the screen.

Dr. Hess mutes the TV and turns toward Cloris.

"What was that all about?" She asked.

"I got a call about an hour ago requesting a copy of the fingerprints we have on file from Mary Hororwitz." Hess was sweating and sounded out of breath. "As I was looking for them I saw the newscast. Well, as it turns out, the prints we have on file match the fingerprints at all of the attacks. The Sheriff's Department and the State Police have ID'd the prints as Mary's."

"That can't be! It's not true!" Nurse Cloris blurted out. "I saw her, I was there! She was dead!" Cloris went pale.

"Somehow she's back." Hess said fearfully.

"What do we do?" Cloris put her hand on his should and started to visibly shake.

The lights abruptly flickered and then went out all together.

"Oh my God!" Cloris shouted.

The lights began to flicker like a strobe, and the door that Dr. Hess had closed and locked burst open without warning, shards of the wooden frame flying all over the room. Standing in the doorway, laughing in the flickering light, was Mary.

"Mary?" Dr. Hess shouted. "Is that really you?"

Mary answered him with more laughter and a slash across the chest from the cleaver. The doctor fell to the floor, gushing blood. Clorise screamed and ran for the door, but Mary grabbed her arm and spun her around.

'Thanks for taking care of me so well you bitch!' She thought, swinging the cleaver down hard on Cloris' head. It sounded like a ripe melon being smashed. Mary let the body fall to the floor next to Dr. Hess who was still shouting. She yanked out the cleaver and silenced Dr. Hess.

TEN

Michael Chadwick, still in town, was on his way home after picking up take-out from a Chinese Restaurant on 'Mary Horror Night'. After the incident at Gravestone Hospital he was a mess. He got so drunk that night at JC's Pub that the Sheriff drove him home.

Dealing with the Sheriff had suddenly become easy ever since they discussed splitting the advance on Michael's next book; which would be about Mary Horowitz with the Sheriff playing a major role in it as the person that found her and her family.

While he was getting drunk with the Sheriff, he spoke to him off the cuff about a few of the things Mary said when he saw her; like how she never went home after being patched up at the regular hospital, and how she was only questioned once about the murders, and only by him. The Sheriff turned it all around into Mary being a raving lunatic and went so far as to say she attacked him and the staff at the hospital.

Nothing the Sheriff said added up. Mary couldn't have moved from her bed much less attack anyone with a belly wound the way the EMT's described it.

The next day, after sobering up, Michael started digging deep into everything he could to find to learn as much as possible about the Horowitz family, and their life before the murders. One of the interesting things he found out after paying off someone from the coroner's office was the lack of photographic evidence regarding Jeff Horowitz's body. There were pictures for the other family members in their autopsy files, but not his, and the photo used for Arleen Horowitz was badly out of date, and shouldn't have been used for her file. With the way things had been written up, Chadwick wouldn't have been surprised to see it all in crayon.

He was going to attempt to discuss it with Sheriff Tom on a night when he had too much to drink, but he got word that Mary Horowitz had killed herself only a few hours after he'd seen her the day before.

"So I was out getting shitfaced while she killed herself," he said to himself in his motel room after hearing the news. He wanted to drink again and try to forget about his role in her death, but decided against it. The guilt he felt made him even more determined to find out what really happened. If it turned out that Mary was actually insane and murdered her family, great, fine and dandy, he'd write his book the way he originally intended, but if not, he wanted to bring the news to the public whether he profited by it or not.

He had serious doubts as to Mary being insane, and he felt horrible that she was dead. If she hadn't killed herself, and he was able to prove she was innocent, she might have been freed and able to at least have a chance at a normal life. He was going to visit the memorial service, but decided against it. Michael thought that he didn't belong there until he could figure things out and hopefully, if his hunches were correct, ultimately clear her of her families' murder.

Michael was getting out of his car with his bag of Chinese when he heard someone come up behind him in a hurry. He spun, ready to swing with his free hand when he saw that it was his nephew, Fred.

"God, Fred, don't do that," he grinned tightly, "I almost swung at you."

"Sorry Uncle Mike, but I had to see you." Fred sounded stressed.

"I thought you guys moved out of town months ago, what are you doing here?" He asked, walking to his room.

"You need to get out here, it isn't safe anymore." Fred blurted out.

"I don't know what you're talking about, I'm not going anywhere." Michael looked at Fred. "Do your parents know you're even here?"

"Listen, that doesn't matter." There was a sense of urgency to Fred's words and he grabbed Michaels arm, holding it tightly. "Mary is under a spell."

"No, she's dead, and I might be one of the reasons why." He responded coldly.

"No, she's not dead, she's back." He shook his head. "Where have you been all night, haven't you seen the news? People are dying!"

"I haven't watched TV for a couple of days." He tugged his arm free and looked confused. "What the hell are you talking about?"

"It's like I said, Mary is under a spell. It brought her back from the dead so she could kill everyone who wronged her, and that includes you."

"That's not going to scare me away." Michael said firmly.

"Mary meant a lot to me. I loved her, and I didn't even realize it until she was gone. I started looking into what was going on. She's under the spell of that book. The one that they've got on display at the library."

"It's at the library?" He vaguely remembered seeing Mary with a book when he visited her. It looked very old, with a strange symbol on the cover. If it was the same one that would make sense, but how would it end up in the library, he wondered.

"Yeah, I looked into it and found out that Mary is a descendent of Rebecca, the woman who wrote that book. You know what happened to her? She was accused of killing her family, and being a witch. They hunted her down and she was hanged in front of the entire town. She came back and in turn, hunted them down, killed them all and haunted her house. Mary is doing the same thing."

"So you're telling me that Mary's going to come back and hunt down everybody that wronged her?" He asked incredulously. "Murder each of them, and then haunt the house she lived in?"

"Yes." Fred looked at him intensely.

"That still isn't going to scare me away. I have a bit of a problem I have to resolve, and if I don't I could end up dead anyway, so either way -"

Fred held up his hand and cut him off. "There might even be a way to fix this; some counter-spell in the book or something, but you know what, I'm not sticking around to find out. I came to warn you. And by the way, what are you doing? Did you forget why you came here? Did you forget about Kelly like everybody else seems to have?"

"There are a lot of people that I have obligations to, and owe money to. I have a deal going right now with this town and it's going to make that better. That's what I got."

Fred turned and started to walk away. Michael stopped him, firmly gripping his shoulder.

"Tell your mom I didn't forget about Kelly." He said.

"Fuck you!" Fred replied, pulling away.

*****

Sheriff Tom finally woke again. His head was pounding like a jackhammer but he managed to stand, sluggishly making it back to his patrol car. He ignored all the blood inside it, and pulled Andy's body out, letting it fall to the road in a heap. He could still see out of the windshield with his remaining eye, so he started the car and drove off. The radio was still on, with the news confirming that Mayor Grafton had been killed.

"Sorry to hear that Joe," his voice was thick and gravely, "but Sheriff Tom is in charge now!" He stomped on the gas and let the siren scream like a banshee.

*****

Michael showed up at the library after watching a few minutes of the news. It basically confirmed what his nephew Fred had told him with the exclusion of the murders being the result of Mary Horowitz coming back from the dead.

He had to find the book that Fred was talking about.

There were only a few people inside probably because it was 'Mary Horror Night', though he doubted the festivities would continue with all the attacks and murders. He recognized an older woman browsing the periodicals as his sister's old cleaning lady. He ducked around so she couldn't see him just in case he was spotted. Michael didn't want to deal with answering questions about anything, especially Kelly.

He began to roam the aisles in hopes of finding the book that Fred had told him about.

"Excuse me, we're closing in about fifteen minutes, do you need some help?" The librarian asked, pointing to the watch she wore.

"This is probably going sound really weird, but do you have Mary Horror's spell book?" Michael felt slightly embarrassed, thinking she wouldn't even know what he was talking about.

"Well actually we do." She replied, straightening her glasses. "It was donated to the library by Mayor Grafton after she died. It's in local history." She pointed a thumb behind her and smiled.

"Can you show it to me?" He asked.

"You'll have to fill out these forms since you're not on our lending list." The woman said handing him a thin pamphlet of paper. Michael rolled his eyes but filled them out.

She brought him to the book, which was set apart from the rest on its own stand. He immediately recognized it as the same one that

Mary had with her at the asylum. The same she held onto like a prized teddy bear.

"Its signed out to you already, but be careful with it and make sure its back here in two weeks." The librarian warned.

"I will," he rushed past her and headed out.

*****

The first thing that Sheriff Tom wanted to do was secure all the cash from his dealings with Mayor Grafton because he had a bad feeling about the entire situation. If the shit hit the fan and he was implicated in anything he'd need to 'get out of Dodge' quick, and he'd need cash for that.

So with an eye missing, and blood all over his uniform and face, he drove to the Mayor's house, where the cash was being stashed until it was supposed to be divided the following evening after 'Mary Horror Night'.

"Mary Horror," he said pulling into the Mayor's driveway. "I hope I never hear that fucking name again!"

He grabbed the key to the front of the house from the bottom of an artificial rock at the front of the house and let himself in. The safe was over the mantle, behind some of the stonework. He knew the combo, they both did just in case there was ever an emergency. Inside were several envelopes full of cash. From what the Mayor had told him earlier, they had accumulated nearly a half million in cash over the previous quarter.

The Sheriff found on old suitcase and started pulling cash out of envelopes and filling it with neat little stacks of bills. When the safe was empty, he slammed it shut, wiped his fingerprints off and snapped the suitcase shut.

He saw a picture of the mayor standing with his ex-wife and son George on the mantle. His eyes narrowed. "Fifteen percent my ass!" He looked up and saw Grafton's shotgun hanging from wrought iron hooks and yanked it off the wall. "I think I'll take this too, since you won't be needing it!" He stomped out of the house and got back into his patrol car. "Now to see about ending this 'Mary Horror' bullshit once and for all!"

The Sheriff drove into town, and saw people flocking to their cars and leaving. Some of the vending tables had been left unattended, and there were State Troopers at the movie theater. One of the abandoned vending tables caught his eye and he jerked the wheel to the side and pulled over.

Leaving the lights on and the siren going, he walked over to the table. He smirked when he saw the merchandise there. Whoever owned the table had all sorts of props for witches. There were brooms, fake warts, noses, and most importantly, what he needed; a black eye patch. He snatched one up, pulled it free of the wrapper and put it on. Then he got back into his patrol car and sped to the Horowtiz house.

*****

Kim didn't know where else to go after being questioned by Deputy Ted and a couple of State Troopers. They all creeped her out, and she thought one of them might have been trying to look down her shirt.

She couldn't go home because the house was empty. Her parents had left for a weekend getaway, and Kim was long past the age where she'd either have to go with them or get a babysitter.

So she went to Mark's house.

He didn't let her in, which surprised her considering how he used to have the hots for her so badly before he couldn't keep his hands off her.

"So why are you here?" He gestured to the front steps. "Have a seat."

Kim thought back a few hours to when she watched Mary practically gut George, and then she heard about what happen to his father and the others. It was so overwhelming, she started to cry.

"I just didn't want to be alone, and I didn't have anyone else to turn to right now." She said, wiping her eyes.

"Why?" Mark asked, confused.

"Because George is dead!" she stammered.

"Oh come on." Mark sounded casual, shaking his head with a half-smile on his face. "You know all the stuff that's going on, everything on the news; it's all probably just a publicity stunt. George and his father are probably behind everything and it'll come out sometime tomorrow that everyone is okay." He chuckled. "George's dad has been crazy with the whole 'Mary Horror' thing since it all started way back with the homecoming game, when we were all still in high school."

"No, no," her hands trembled when she touched his arm, trying to convince him. "I was there! I saw her. It was her, really her! She's back. I don't know how, but she's back!"

"Saw who?" Mark was totally confused. "Who's back? What the hell are you talking about?"

"Mary. She killed him. She killed George. I saw it happen right in front of me!" She burst into tears and held on to him. "She's back!"

"That's impossible. Mary's dead." He gently pushed her off and looked her in the eyes and spoke calmly. "Mary's dead. She killed herself."

"No, she's not." Kim insisted. Her whole body began to shake. "I saw her and she killed George. She chased me! She chased me outside! She was gonna kill me too if she ever caught up to me!"

"Alright, calm down, please." He took off his jacket and swung it around Kim's shoulders then he held her close trying to calm her sobs away. "Listen, I don't know if you heard, but my family is moving to Florida. They're out there now, so you should spend the night here."

"Are you sure?" She was still sobbing against him.

"We're both alone. My parents aren't around and they're not going to be back for a few days. By then all this should just be a memory." He looked into her eyes. "Stay here with me. You'll be safe here. Everything will feel better in the morning."

"Okay," she agreed, and Mark kissed her lightly on the forehead.

Mark helped her to her feet and the two of them went inside.

They settled on the landing upstairs, and looked through the window across from them where they could see the moon and the stars. Mark slipped his jacket off Kim and started to rub her shoulders.

"I'll show you where the spare bedroom is." He said, and brought her to a small room with a folding bed against the far wall and a few non-descript pieces of furniture. Kim sat on the bed and smacked the spot next to her, inviting him to sit with her.

Mark rubbed her shoulders again, feeling the tension ease.

"So, are you gonna miss when I move down there to Florida?" he said, half joking.

"Yeah, I will." She sounded slightly embarrassed. "And because I kind of want to get out of here too. I don't want to be here anymore."

"Well, once I get down there and get things going, maybe enroll in college, start playing football down there, you can come see me or even move down there." He said nervously. The last thing he needed was rejection. He hadn't let himself get close to anyone since the whole situation with Mary happened.

"That sounds like a good idea." Kim replied, a little hesitant.

"Really? Yeah?" he was pleasantly surprised, especially when she turned to him and pushed him down on the bed.

They started kissing and Mark was feeling great, like he was in heaven, and then somewhere along the way he lost it, and remembered Mary. He's still kissing Kim, but now he smells Mary's perfume. He opens his eyes and sees that it's Mary he's kissing, not Kim. His eyes bug out and he jumps backwards on the bed, shoving Kim away from him.

"Mark!" Kim shouted. "What the hell is your problem?" She sat forward, leaning toward him.

Mark sat there out of breath and pale as a ghost. He shook his head in an attempt to clear it, but still had the eerie sensation of Mary being with him and not Kim. For a second he squeezed his eyes shut and forced himself to be okay, to calm down, because Mary was dead and not anywhere near his house.

"Nothing's wrong, I'm sorry," he tried to sound calm, but failed miserably.

"No, what is wrong." Kim put her hand on his arm.

"Nothing, I'm really sorry." He put his hand on the side of her face and moved closer to kiss her again. "Just forget about it, I'm sorry."

They started to kiss, but Kim pulled away.

"No, really, just tell me what's wrong." She pleaded.

"I'm fine, really." They began kissing again and the door across the hall, Mark's bedroom, slowly closed, then the door to the room they were in suddenly slammed shut.

"What the fuck was that?" Mark said, turning away from Kim to look at the door. He got up and tried the door. It opened without incident, so he stepped into the hall with Kim following close behind.

Holding hands, they made their way to the stairs and started going down. The lights flickered several times, and they stopped each time, with Mark calling out to see if anyone was in the house. When they were finally able to reach the ground floor, Mark checked the front door, and there was no one there. He turned and headed toward the kitchen, still holding Kim's hand and still calling out.

While they were still in the hall leading to the kitchen, the lights began to flicker again, than stopped. Reluctantly, he took another step.

"Do you hear that?" Kim asked nervously.

"I don't hear anything." He replied, looking around from where he stood.

"It sounded like it was coming from in there." Kim pointed to the living room across the hall.

"I'll go check it out." He edged her to the wall and put his hand reassuringly on her shoulder. "You stay here, I'll only be gone a second." Kim nodded trembling slightly.

Kim turned back around and saw the kitchen only a step away. Nervous, she peeked around the corner, saw that there was no one there and stepped into the kitchen. She turned back and was going to walk back into the hall when she saw it there on the table.

Mary Horror's meat cleaver.

The tears came and she cried, not hearing Mark creeping up behind her. He had gone the full circle around the living room and seen nothing, so he came into the kitchen from the other side.

"Boo!" He said into her ear.

Kim screamed and nearly jumped through the roof. She was still in tears, and slapped Mark hard on the arm.

"Why would you do that?" she said angrily.

"I'm sorry, chill out, really, I'm sorry." Mark held her close for a second then pulled away. "I didn't mean to scare you like that."

"I hated when you used to do that to me in school but now it's even worse with what's going on!" she hit her thigh with a fist.

"It was just a little joke." He noticed she'd been crying. "What happened, what's wrong?"

Look-" she pointed to the cleaver. "It's Mary's cleaver."

"What are you talking about, that's my mom's cleaver." He said, adding with a chuckle, "She uses that to make pork chops."

"No, that's her cleaver." She insisted.

A low moaning sound echoed through the kitchen, sounding like 'Mark'.

"You heard that this time right?" Kim said, hoping he did.

"Yeah, and it sounded like my name. C'mon," he took her hand and led her back through the living room.

The lights blinked several times again, and suddenly Mary Horror was standing in the corner of the living room smiling at them both.

"Kim run, get out of here!" Mark made a mad dash for the front door with Kim only a step behind. He threw open the door and ran across the street, standing on the grass next to a large oak tree.

"Are you okay?" He asked Kim.

"Yeah. Did you see her follow us?" Kim was frantically looking around, but saw nothing.

"No, but she had to have." Mark looked at the house. The lights were off and the door was closed, but neither of them closed the door. "Maybe you should go back inside and try to hide. Get your phone and call the police. I'm going to look around out here." He turned and started to run, but slammed right into Mary, and fell flat.

Mary made a growling sound, smacking Mark on the side of his head with the flat of the cleaver, knocking him out. Kim turned just in time to see Mary hit Mark with the blade. While her back was turned,

Kim ran and jumped on her back, wrapping an arm around her neck in an attempt to choke her.

"Why are you doing this you sick freak!" Kim screamed at her, tightening her grip.

Mary just laughed and swung her arm backwards as hard as she could, hitting Kim right in the face with her elbow and knocking her to the ground. Both Mark and Kim were unconscious, lying at her feet. Mary looked up at the stars and shrieked.

*****

The book felt warm in Michael's hands. He dropped it on the passenger seat and drove away from the library unable to keep his thoughts away from what might be inside it. The curiosity was maddening, and he ended up parking on the side of the road, turning the interior light on.

"Let's see what this is all about." He said flipping the book open and started skimming through it. He started reading aloud random sentences here and there, until he found the spell she must have used.

"Make the correct incision and say the spell words repeatedly. 'Call me by name, I will rise again from the witches blood I came. If

the body dies, the soul will reanimate itself as the way it sees itself'."
Michael shook his head, still staring in the book. "Oh my god, she turned herself into a fuckin' zombie!"

He thought about the money he could get from the book alone if he just up and ran, but then he started to think about the whole picture, and realized that having someone like Mary around would mean he could write the book and it would have credibility. He could pay off all the debt he owed and finally have a fresh start without having to be concerned with one of Lloyd's men breaking his legs. There it was again, the problem that loomed over everything. He may have put out a great children's book, but he was for all intents and purposes broke because he owed and hadn't been able to pay it back. Now he had an opportunity to do just that.

He took out his phone and hit Lloyd's number.

"Lloyd," he said to the person on the other end. "This is Michael Chadwick."

"Michael Chadwick?" the man on the other end said. "I haven't heard from you in too long of a time! You got my money?"

"Yes, I've got it totally under control. There's this zombie chick running around and killing everybody."

"What? What the hell are you talking about?" Lloyd said, really just wanting to hear about when he was going to get paid.

"You're going to get everything that you're looking for. I've got officials on my side and she's just gonna slice up all of them. I'm gonna have a story-"

"What? I just want my money!" Lloyd was getting angry listening to all of his bullshit. "I'm hanging up. Just call me when you want to drop off the cash!"

The phone went dead in his hand, but it didn't bother him, because he knew he was in a great position at the moment. He could do something great for Mary by helping her and he could also help himself by selling the story and paying off his debt.

He thought it was a win-win situation, and headed toward Mary's house hoping to take a few moody pictures to add to the coming story.

ELEVEN

Mark was lying on his stomach when he started to wake up. It was a struggle at first, his head and face hurt beyond belief, and he just wanted to go back to sleep until the pain went away. The last thing he remembered was seeing Mary swing the cleaver at him. Against his better judgment he lifted his head up and looked around. Through the dizziness and nauseous feeling he saw that he was still in the woods. He spotted blonde hair a few feet away and knew that it had to be Kim. She was with him, and still knocked out, or worse, because he couldn't see all of her from where he was lying.

Flipping over made him want to puke, and so did pushing himself back so his back was against the oak tree across the street from his house. He touched the side of his face and winced. There was swelling, but it wasn't as bad as he expected. He guessed that he had a concussion, and tried to look around more without moving too fast. That was when she came into view.

Mary saw that Mark was awake and moving. She congratulated herself for not hitting him too hard and killing him.

"What do you want?" Mark whispered as she grew near.

Mary was silent, and knelt down facing him. Slowly, she brought her face to his, and she kissed him. She kissed him like they used to kiss when they were still a couple, when she was still alive.

Suddenly, they were at the Homecoming Dance. They were in the center of the dance floor, and there was no one else around. He was holding her close and happy, skin tingling at her touch, breathing in the scent of her hair and perfume and loving the way they were dancing slowly and kissing.

"We had our dance, now it's time to pay for it." Mark heard Mary's voice in his head, and it sounded like hot gravel getting water poured on it.

Mark's eyes flipped open just in time to see Mary plunge her hand right into his chest. He lost consciousness as she ripped out his heart and tossed it on the ground right in front of Kim's face. Mary laughed, long and hard. She giggled like a little girl when Kim was startled awake.

Kim woke up horrified at the heart lying only inches from her face. She jerked herself to her knees, saw Mark sitting back against the tree with a hole in his chest and she shrieked, pushing herself to stand and run. She ran as fast as she could, head still spinning, and stomach lurching with every speedy stride. She ran through the woods, not sure where she was anymore, and then she came to the house.

It was bright yellow, the color amplified but the light of the full moon and stars. She stopped running, putting her hands on her knees while she panted, and dreaded going inside the house before her. She knew who's house it was. She remembered that Mark had told her Mary was his neighbor.

There was a rustling in the bushes close behind her, so she threw caution to the wind and ran to Mary's house, racing up the porch steps and grabbing the door knob. She tried twisting it, but it was locked. She jumped the stairs and headed around to the back. To her utter surprise, the door flung open when she turned the knob.

Kim flung the door shut and made sure it was locked behind her. Then she ran through the kitchen, aside from a strange looking envelope sitting on the counter, it was mostly empty, nothing there to use as a weapon. She frantically ran into the dining room and tripped up on the leg of a chair, falling hard. Before she could stand up completely, she lifted her head up and saw shoes. Mary was there, standing directly in front of her. Her laughter filled the room with a chilling monstrous sound.

"You bitch!" Kim blurted out as she tried to stand. Before she could, Mary swung the cleaver. In one swift movement Mary had cut her head clean off her shoulders. With a spray of blood, her still twitching body hit the floor with a dull thud, her head rolling by Mary's feet. The angry expression would forever be locked on Kim's face.

There was silence afterward, and Mary stood there looking around the room, noting how everything was just as it was before her family had died. 'So much is the same, yet everything is different.' She thought to herself.

The sound of keys jingling broke the silence. Someone was at the front door. Mary couldn't imagine who it could be, thinking she'd already taken care of the Mayor and the Sheriff, who were running the house as a tourist attraction.

She heard the door rattle and saw the knob turn as if it were in slow motion. When the door swung open, the figure behind it was shrouded in the shadows of the night.

"Hello-" The shrouded figure called out, closing the door.

Mary was familiar with the voice, but hearing it sent her back to the nightmare she had while still in the hospital shortly after being stabbed.

"Mary?" It was her father's voice, and indeed it was he who stood in front of her, dressed neatly in a suit and tie.

"Mary?" he repeated in amazement, stepping forward. "But you're dead. What happened to you? What-" He sees the bloodied cleaver held loosely in her hand, and looking further spots the head on the floor. "Oh my god!" He lunged backward, holding his hands up toward her. "Calm down Mary, just calm down. You're probably just really confused right now, and I can understand why." Terrified, he stuttered and paced backward, further down the hallway and into the house. "You probably thought that I was dead and that Kelly was still missing right? You see? You're not right inside. I'm still alive, and Kelly, she's outside waiting for me."

Mary wasn't hearing any of it. She just saw a man in front of her that had basically thrown her away to be tortured for the rest of her life, with the reputation of a psychotic killer forever hanging over her head. She gazed at her father with a twisted grin, and slightly raised the cleaver in his direction.

"Look, it wasn't supposed to be this way." He stumbled over his words, still trying to reach her somehow. "Things got out of hand. It started out as just a plan between the Mayor, the Sheriff and I to make some money. We were all having some money problems and the town was ready to fall flat too. We were going to make our own little Salem over here. Remember when we lived in Salem, and how the tourists used to flock there year after year and spend all their money? Well, why couldn't we do that here?"

Mary slowly edged up on him, and he started to back up again, his words spoken even more quickly, like staccato bursts of attempted reasoning, but coming out more like the pleas of a broken man, the pleas of a man about to die.

"All we had to do was create a legend, a myth. All we needed was our own little witch or psycho, like Lizzy Borden." He started to gasp, his heart pounding so hard and fast in his chest that he thought he was going to fall over. Mary was still walking forward to him, edging him further backwards until the back of his feet hit the staircase leading to the upper floor. He started backing his way up the stairs. "You were perfect for what we needed. You always carried that spell book around. You even come from a family of witches. And let's not forget, you were emotionally depressed from your best friend vanishing." He had to pause for a moment to catch his breath, still struggling to find words. "You were on antidepressants and borderline suicidal." He reached the landing at the top of the stairs and was backed into the wall. Mary raised the cleaver a little higher.

"Okay, it was Kelly's idea! She's the one that killed them!" He shouted, holding his hand up to fend her off. "I was sleeping with her. I know that probably sounds disgusting but it was all because of your mother. She was leaving me!" He tripped himself up and fell with his back against the wall. "Oh my god, Mary, what have you become?"

"Mary Horror!" She whispered, a hairs breath from his face.

She decided that cutting him was too easy, so her hand let go of the cleaver and it dropped to the floor at her side. She put her hands on her father's chest and he screamed in terror. Her fingers sunk into his flesh. Her father's eyes rolled until the white showed clearly, and he stopped struggling as she began ripping his skin apart until she was able to snap open his ribcage and tear out the organs within, grabbing his heart and crushing it in her hands. Blood was everywhere. She was covered in it, and he father lay there, literally an empty dead man.

Kelly was dressed to the nines, leaning against the back of the BMW outside smoking a cigarette. She resented having to be there, annoyed that it was taking so long just to pick up an envelope of money. She wanted to be long gone from what she considered a 'little hick town in the middle of nowhere' and back in the city where they belonged. It didn't matter in the city if their wealth came from the life insurance of a dead wife and son, or that her man was over twice her age. With their new identities nothing of their past applied anymore except when they picked up their cut of the Mayor's business venture.

She didn't hear any screams from inside the house, and had no idea that Jeff Horowitz had been literally taken apart and brutally murdered. She was so into thinking of herself that she would never have thought that Mary was back from the dead, much less approaching her from behind.

Suddenly the wind picked up, and Kelly heard her name being whispered behind her. For a second, she thought it might just be the wind whistling through the trees, but then she heard it louder, closer. She stepped away from the car, turning to see Mary smiling at her.

"Oh shit!" Kelly put her hand over her mouth, wanting to gag at the sight of the gray skinned Mary, dressed in her homecoming gown and covered in blood.

Mary laughed wickedly, holding the cleaver that had become the trademark of 'Mary Horror Night' over her head. Kelly never expected to see the real thing.

"Wait!" Kelly shouted. "I can explain!"

Mary was on before she could utter another word. The cleaver came down, hacking a deep gash at the base of Kelly's throat. Blood squirted upward and she fell to the ground in front of the car. She tried to push herself up, but collapsed. Mary grinned and walked back toward the house.

Michael Chadwick pulled up to Mary's house seconds later. The car skidded to a halt when he spotted the body on the side of the road.

"My god, that's Kelly!" He shouted, leaping out of his vehicle. He ran to her side, the spell book falling out of his hands along the way. He was sobbing when he saw all the blood. The wound she had said it all. "No, what did she do to you?" he cried, holding her close. "I should never have gotten involved in any of this!" he proclaimed, screaming Mary's name.

She was there a moment later, growling at him like a rabid dog.

"Mary," he said quietly. "Not you, not now." He said, running off into the woods along the same path that she had run two years earlier.

Mary followed, never breaking stride, not bothering to run because no matter what, certain that she would get him one way or another.

The Sheriff raced through the woods, shotgun in hand. He wanted to get to Mary's house unseen so he could pick up the money that rightly belonged to Jeff, and hopefully run into Mary Horror along the way so he could put a bullet in her head and end the misery she'd begun by coming back to life.

Sheriff Tom got to the house just in time to see Mary chasing Michael Chadwick into the woods. He followed, knowing he'd either take them both down or at least whoever was left after they had their own personal stand-off, and then come back for the money.

"You don't have to do this, really, you don't." Michael said breathlessly stumbling through the woods. "I was never your enemy. I was only trying to help you, not hurt you. I didn't know what really happened, what they did to you!"

Mary didn't say a word. She liked being quiet around the people that hurt her or hoped to gain something by her pain and death. They said such wonderfully foolish things in hopes of saving their own wretched lives.

Michael stumbled backwards, his back at the base of thick tree.

"Put it down," he cried, "you don't have to do this, put it down, put it down."

But Mary kept coming forward.

"Drop the cleaver Mary!" Sheriff Tom said, pointing his shotgun at her.

"Sheriff, help me!" Michael shouted. "Sheriff, please!"

Sheriff Tom looked back and forth between Michael and Mary, settling on Michael. He leveled the shotgun and squeezed the trigger. Michael's head slammed back against the tree in a splatter of blood and mangled brains.

Mary stared at Michael, lying there dead, and then turned to the Sheriff.

"It's all good?" he asked, nodding to Michael. "An eye for an eye?"

Mary shrugged her shoulders but made no move against him.

Sheriff Tom turned around and headed back to the house, where he still had some money to pick up.

"Fucking zombie she-bitch!" he muttered under his breath.

Mary heard him and threw the cleaver hard and fast. It sunk into his back and the Sheriff fell flat on his face. She yanked it free afterward and walked back to her house. Along the way she found the spell book, feeling its warmth, she took it with her. The house looked as if it glowed, much the same as it did the night her family died. She stood facing it and staring at the book, realizing how closely its story, Rebecca's story, came to her own.

Suddenly she heard her name being called out.

"Mary," it was the sound of her mother's voice. "Come home Mary."

Mary looked up from the book and saw the ghost image of her mother and grandmother standing in front of the house. It was like they were waiting for her there.

"Mary, it's time to leave the evil behind." Her grandmother said.

"Come inside Mary, your brother is waiting for you." Her mother said.

"Come home Mary, you did what needed to be done." Her grandmother said.

Mary could feel the love they had for her, and it eased her hunger for vengeance. Her battles were over, so she followed home. She silently vowed to never leave her house again.

Epilogue

Sheriff Tom felt rage building inside him, overriding the pain from the fresh wound in his back. He rose from the ground and howled in the night like a tormented angry beast!

 Nick Kisella grew up in Manville, New Jersey, where he began writing fantasy and horror while attending high school. Some of his first published work appeared in the Indie magazines 'Dreadknight', and 'The Nocturnal Lyric'. Since then his work has appeared in various forms from print and online magazines to blogs. His first fantasy novel, 'The Emerald and the Blade' came out in 1989 by a long defunct publisher, with 'The Chalice of Souls' soon to follow.

Some of his more recent work includes a screenplay and novelization for 'Nifty Entertainment' a California based Indie production company, as well as getting the first two fantasy novels he wrote as a teen, 'The Chalice of Souls' and 'Death and the Doomweaver' back in print for the sheer nostalgia of it. 'Morningstars', his first full-length horror novel was published by Black Bed Sheet Books in 2012. 'The Beasts and the Walking Dead' a post-apocalyptic fiction novel, has also been published by Black Bed Sheet Books and is the first part of a series. He wrote the novelization to the James Balsamo film, 'I Spill Your Guts', and recently finished penning the novelization for the Ryan Scott Weber film, 'Mary Horror'. Always having an eventful life, he writes when time allows, usually after dark.

A fitness enthusiast, he has been a certified fitness instructor involved in the industry for twenty years, and continues to stay in shape and train individuals while well into his 40s.

Nick resides in rural Northwestern New Jersey with his wife and twins.

Ryan Scott Weber (Born February 24, 1980) is an American film director, screenwriter, producer, cinematographer, actor, editor and musician. He shoots and produces many of his films in his native town of Bernardsville, New Jersey. Ryan began his interest in filmmaking at just 15 years old with an old VHS camcorder. Now, at the age of 33, he is the owner of Weber Pictures Company in New Jersey. Weber also plays the drums and has released two albums with the Trustkill Records band Crash Romeo in 2006 and 2008. For almost 15 years now he is still directing, editing, writing, producing, acting, drumming and shooting. Weber has a distinctive directorial style. He manages to make what looks like big budget movies for little money. Weber's first feature film, Mary Horror, was released in 2012 and he has recently completed the sequel Sheriff Tom Vs. The Zombies. Weber is a strong supporter of independent film and the conventions that are involved in this surrounding. Weber and his crew have attended and ventured over ten conventions in the last year and in October 2012; The Chiller Theatre Convention in Parsippany, NJ featured the film Mary Horror with two exclusive showings. Weber will continue to make independent films and ensures us the best in yet to come!